TABLE D'HOTE
DOUGLAS CLARK

Also available in Perennial Library by Douglas Clark:

TABLE D'HOTE

DOUGLAS CLARK

PERENNIAL LIBRARY
Harper & Row, Publishers
New York, Cambridge, Philadelphia, San Francisco
London, Mexico City, São Paulo, Singapore, Sydney

For Sheila and Len Moor
who lent me the fabric of Jackdaws
to re-erect far away as Pilgrim's

A hardcover edition of this book was published by Victor Gollancz Ltd.
It is here reprinted by arrangement with the author.

First PERENNIAL LIBRARY edition published 1984.

Library of Congress in Publication Data

Clark, Douglas.
  Table d'hôte.

  I. Title.
PR6053.L294T3 1984   823'.914   84-47665
ISBN 0-06-080723-7 (pbk.)

84 85 86 87 88 10 9 8 7 6 5 4 3 2 1

TABLE D'HOTE

Chapter 1

THE RESTAURANT WAS a secretive place in so far as it was difficult to find without precise instructions as to how to get there. There was no sign post on the main road to suggest that the Bramblebush was just round the corner, tucked away, its front hidden by the jutted building line of the antique dealer's shop. And the little side road itself came into the main road at the wrong angle to encourage passing trade. For those speeding away from London it angled away backwards, hairpinning left to obscure even the view of interested passengers. For those coming into London it posed a difficult right turn across heavy traffic, to lead to what ... ?

You had to get there to find out. A board on the boundary wall of the property told customers there was a car park at the rear. Then, almost apologetically, the word Restaurant had been added. Anybody unfamiliar with the house would not know whether the arrow indicating the way to the car park also pointed to the restaurant, or whether the two messages had been ill-designed and so had become misleading where they were meant to guide.

Wanda Mace had realised she was close to the turn-off because the instructions David Bymeres had given her were precise. "When you reach the triangular patch of green, you're there. Coast along until you reach the end of it and then turn right. The Bramblebush is only twenty yards down the side road. Pass it and turn left into the car park."

She did as she had been told. The little lead-in to the car park ran past the open door of what was obviously a kitchen area, past a neatly stacked heap of beer crates and white metal barrels, and then turned on to a surprisingly large apron of tarmac laid out geometrically with broad white lines to indicate parking spaces for eighteen or twenty cars. There were probably a dozen already there, but David's yellow Renault 17 was easy to pick out. She slipped the Mini into an empty space beside it, nosing the bonnet up to a low wall of peat blocks where skilful gardening had resulted in a cascade of blue lobelia fronting a raised border of South African marigolds, multi-coloured petunias and clumps of purple phlox. It was all so neat and colourful, without being twee, that she sat for a moment to admire it. She would have liked to see a honeysuckle on the old wall behind the bed. She thought it a pity to have such a south-facing expanse without making use of it. Perhaps a cordon-pear, apple, cherry or even more exotic fruits—peach or a grape-vine.

There was a light tap on the roof of the Mini. Not the soft tap of finger ends, but the sharper sound of finger nails. David! She could see in her mind's eye the well-kept finger nails playing the little drum roll. He had exquisite nails, very rounded at the ends, and worn slightly longer than most men. She remembered an occasion a few weeks ago when she had sat up in bed to polish her own nails, with David beside her, still asleep. One of his hands had been on top of the coverlet. In a love-urged gesture she had lifted it and started to buff the nails. It had wakened him, but he had lain there, quite still, allowing her to continue. While he had been asleep it had seemed merely an indication of affection on her own part, but after he had woken and made no effort to withdraw the hand, she had wondered whether vanity had not caused his acquiescence. Always vanity! She supposed all men had a flaw. With David, she had never discovered any, other than vanity. Vanity about clothes, his professional expertise, his skill at love-making. . . .

"How about it then?" His face appeared at her open window. "Are you going to spend all day dreaming?"

She leaned sideways and upwards to kiss him before opening the door. Getting out was a business. The adjacent vehicle was too close. But she knew she looked good, and could almost feel David's appreciative gaze as she angled out, long legs foremost. Million-dollar legs, he called them. He was even vain about how expensive his women's bodies looked.

8

She was in a brown linen dress, cut square and moderately low at the neck. She had chosen it not to set off her tan, but rather to match it and to emphasise the almost bleached fairness of her hair, which she wore long. As she locked the car door, he said: "You found it all right, then?"

"I'm here, aren't I?" She felt disappointed. No comment on her appearance. No stroking verbal caress of compliment or pleasure at her arrival.

The notice board had been right. The entrance to the restaurant was at the rear. David led the way off the tarmac and along a narrow path of paving stones across a little lawn no bigger than a billiard table to the door of a small vestibule. It was cool in there. The walls were cream washed and the single refectory table and wall bench shone with the patina of age. Somebody—Wanda guessed at whoever had done the garden—had placed a row of upright bamboos across the recesses on either side of the chimney breast and had trained variegated trailing ivy up to the low ceiling. She liked the atmosphere.

"May we have a drink in here? Just the two of us?"

He looked at his watch. "You're just a bit late. I've a clinic at a quarter past two."

She tucked her handbag under her arm as a gesture of agreement that they should go straight to the table. He led the way without comment. Through the little room and left-about, up a step into the dining room. Wanda felt a pang of disappointment. The room itself was basically attractive, but somebody had found it necessary to do it up. The beams were still there, but the ceiling had been covered with some sort of tiles so that air extractors could be fitted in regimented rows. The tables and chairs were modern reproductions, with upholstery in bright red vinyl. Nor had the interior decorator foresworn the bogus horse-brasses and miniature warming pans which clutter so much lovely stud-work in old houses.

The head-waiter was small, very neat, and half Italian. "This way, doctor, please. And madame!" He led the way to a table at the far end of the room, well away from the other score or so people who were having lunch. After he

9

had tucked her chair in behind her and left the menus, Wanda said: "You seem to be well known here, David."

He smiled—almost smirked. It irritated her. She was surprised enough by her own feelings to wonder why. Perhaps she had been a little put out by the rebuke that she was late for their appointment and had thereby done them out of a pre-lunch drink. But she didn't really think that was it? It was David's attitude. Was she becoming obsessed with his vanity? Seeing it where it didn't exist? In his every action and gesture? Hadn't that comment of hers about him being well known to the head-waiter tickled his vanity? Did even a thing as small as that pander to it? She decided it did. As she glanced through the menu she wondered whether she was going off David a bit. They hadn't seen as much of each other these last three months as formerly. Had that been her decision, or his? Was he losing interest in her? She'd not considered this before now, but it seemed highly probable. The question, if she was right, was why? She made no demands of him. She was, she knew, a personable woman, but ... but what? Well, she was no great beauty. Just average, made to look that much better by careful dressing, and she was thirty-two now, rising thirty-three. A good thirty-three though. It wasn't as if she'd had children to sag her figure, to draw worry lines on her face or to ruin her hands with everlasting nappy washes. Still. . . .

"I can recommend the consommé." It was said without a glance up from the menu. He'd thrown it at her, perhaps helpfully, perhaps dictatorially. She couldn't quite decide. One thing she did know, and that was that she must stop this mental criticism of David or else end the relationship. And in spite of her doubts of the past few minutes she knew that to break with him would be almost impossible for her. She cared too much. Vain or not, he was a damned good lover.

"One thing I've always remembered about you, David. Right from the time when you, Daphne and I first met. You've always liked consommé. You still do apparently."

He laid his menu aside. "I can't stand thick soups."

10

"For medical reasons?"

"Not really. For many years before I decided to become a doctor. Though there are clinical reasons. What goes in at the mouth comes out in the flesh, and you'd be surprised how many patients I see who are obese in the clinical sense."

"I suppose lush, thick soups do add to the ounces. Cream of tomato! I wonder just how much of that is eaten, with all the fattening cornflour or whatever they use to put body in it?"

"When I was much younger...."

"Is this a reminiscence or a reason for disliking thick soup?"

She thought she saw a slight frown of annoyance at the interruption, but he replied readily enough.

"Both. When I was a child, my father used to eat and enjoy certain foods which were prepared especially for men. It was the custom with some old boys."

"Patum peperium? Gentleman's relish?"

"That sort of thing."

"The patum used to come in those lovely heavy pots with loose lids. Like milky glass."

He made no comment on her remembering such things, but ploughed straight ahead with his story. Another thought struck her as she listened. He appeared nervous. Was it because this was their first real meeting in public close to his own home and practice?

"One of the things available in those days was a gentleman's consommé essence. It was a dark brown fluid. Two tablespoons in a pint of clear stock were supposed to delight the men of the family, but women-folk—according to the blurb on the label—would generally not find it to their taste."

"They'd be found guilty of discrimination between the sexes if they were to say that today."

"Maybe. Anyhow, my father used to have it. It was specially made for him while the rest of us had Brown Windsor or whatever the soup of the day happened to be. I can still remember how proud I was when I was given my first serving of father's consommé. I couldn't have disliked it even if it

11

had tasted like dishwater laced with boot polish. I felt then that I was a man at last. I think I was seven at the time."

She smiled at him. "So now, psychologically, you're hooked on clear soup. It must be some form of virility symbol to you."

He nodded. "There may be something in that. But we have such excellent foods in beef and yeast extracts. Good nourishing foods that hardly have a calorie to the pint. They—and good stock—should be used as the ingredients of soup."

"I'll remember that."

"Do. It's a good hint."

"Right. I'll have the consommé and a crab salad."

"Fine."

"Are you having the same?"

"I've eaten so much salad this last week or two I feel I could hire myself out as a pub sign for the Green Man."

"Is Daphne low again?" She asked it tentatively, not sure how he would take this enquiry about his wife. But he seemed relieved to hear she had introduced the subject.

"No more so than usual, but you know how she dotes on tennis, and during the Wimbledon fortnight she never produces anything that means she has to leave the TV set to prepare it. So salad it is, every day and twice a day."

"Poor David!" She put her hand on his across the table. He left it there just long enough to register her touch before picking up the menu again.

"So . . . I'm torn between the pâté and the dish of the day."

"Liver and bacon? In this weather?"

"I dote on it, my sweet. Liver, I mean."

"Now why didn't I know that? I've . . . I mean, we've. . . ."

"Known each other for years and done quite a bit of going to bed together? And despite all this you didn't know I liked liver and bacon? Is that it?"

"More or less." She smiled again. "Strange that one can know so little about a person with whom one is so very friendly."

"Intimately friendly?" This time it was he who stretched out his hand for hers.

12

After a moment—

"Darling, should you? Hold my hand? One of your patients might see you." There was no protest in her voice. Her doubts had gone. David seemed to have recovered from his bout of nervousness. She decided that she had been imagining things. This luncheon, here, in this restaurant, was a new departure for them, and though it was nothing but a delight for her, the implications could just conceivably be serious for him.

"Not in here, they won't. We're four miles from my surgery and so nicely tucked away out of sight that nobody who doesn't live in the immediate neighbourhood would know about it."

"You're not local."

"But I'm one of the people who goes out of his way...."

"To find good places to eat?"

"That—and to find dishy women." He lifted her hand and leaned forward to kiss it.'

"Darling, please! Be careful."

He let the hand go and smiled at her. He was feeling very pleased with himself. The faint feeling of unease he had at the outset was gone. This little party was going off better than he had hoped.

"As long as you're not one of my patients even the B.M.A. cannot frown on my conduct." He said it gaily, almost carelessly.

"Not officially." Now it was her turn to be serious. "But what about Daphne? Does she suspect?"

He frowned a warning that the head-waiter was approaching. The conversation died.

"Are you ready to order, doctor?"

"We'll both have consommé. Then crab salad for one, and I'll have liver and bacon."

"Vegetables, sir?"

"What about some of your delectable whole broad beans? They're on, aren't they?"

"Yes, sir. And some new potatoes?"

"Just right. Can you leave me the wine list?"

As soon as the little black-clad man had swirled away, Wanda asked quietly: "Does Daphne suspect?"

"She suspects all right."

"David! I'm supposed to be her great friend."

"Oh, she doesn't suspect you." He said it airily.

"What then?'

"Simply that I go with another woman." As he said the words, the feeling that it tickled his vanity to be considered a Lothario by his wife returned strongly to her mind.

"Thank heaven for that! Anybody in particular?"

This time he grinned widely. She thought he was a handsome devil. The thought came vividly to her how often she had held his face in her hands and drawn him down....

Her thoughts were interrupted. "Funnily enough, Daphne thinks it is Miss Hector, our practice secretary. Poor Miss Hector! I haven't a clue as to what passions she nurtures in her bosom, but I can assure you that a yearning for me is not among them. I rather think she fancies Roberts, our second senior partner. He's a widower, you see, and so is available in Miss Hector's eyes. Consequently it is not a sin to hunger after him."

"Whereas you, as a married man, are out of reach and so must be out of mind?"

"At a guess, yes."

She wondered. If Miss Hector was a decent sort of woman, she would mother a man like David—if she liked him enough to do so. But from David's tone, she had gathered that the Hector woman didn't like him. If this were so, the question was—why? David was not at the top of the group practice tree, but he was the bright boy among the eight doctors in the group. That, at least, she knew to be true. She had known David and Daphne for years and was well aware of his academic and clinical record. It was good. Of that there was no doubt.

"I shall order half a bottle of hock to go with your crab and chianti for myself. Does that sound all right to you?"

"Perfect. Is chianti one of your great loves, too?"

"Would I be fool enough to drink a wine I didn't like?"

"I've known you order wine on many occasions, but I can't recall chianti."

"Simply, my sweet, because usually I'm choosing a wine for communal drinking. If we were to have just one wine for both of us today I wouldn't choose chianti because it's not to everybody's taste. Some people think it too rough. But it suits me very well."

"You've always indulged your fancies, David."

"Do I detect a note of censure?"

"Of warning."

"About what?"

"Women. Don't be fooled by them, David. I think you would be foolish to suppose—harking back to Miss Hector— that out of reach necessarily means out of mind."

"Thank heaven for that, otherwise you and I. . . ."

He stopped as a waitress brought the consommé. After she had gone he changed the subject. "She's the head-waiter's wife."

"Quite a family affair."

"It is. If they need more than the two of them on duty, her mother helps, and after that, his mother. Both families live in a biggish old house just down the road."

"Mmm ... this is good."

"What were we talking about?"

"David, I think it was a mistake meeting here, so close to your home and practice. I feel so much safer in the cottage a nice, comfortable twelve miles away."

"I know, Wanda. But if we can't meet halfway, we can't meet so often. You must have noticed I haven't seen nearly as much of you recently."

"I still don't think we should take this risk."

He pretended sadness. "I was hoping that if we could establish the Bramblebush as a meeting place for lunch occasionally it would be so very pleasant."

"It would. But lunch is not usually all we want from a meeting, is it?"

"You know it isn't. But when one can't have everything, well, just to sit opposite to you is wonderful."

15

"Thank you, David. I like it, too. But honestly, darling, I feel a bit of a cheat coming here—on to Daphne's doorstep, as it were—to meet her husband. In my own house it seems different. You leave Daphne and come to me."

"Ah, well!"

"And speaking of Daphne, according to your phone call last night she is supposed to be our reason for meeting here today. Or had you forgotten?"

"As if I could!"

"What do you think to my idea of inviting her down to the cottage for a break?"

"You're so thoughtful, Wanda. I think that's one of the reasons why I love you so much." He spoke, or so it seemed to her, with a sense of strain. She wondered whether there wasn't just a touch of false sincerity in his declaration. The thought gave a slight edge to her voice when she replied.

"Does that mean you really do want me to invite her?"

He put his soup spoon down. "Darling, even though I shan't be able to be there, it would mean the most wonderful break for me, too. But I can't help feeling sad at the thought of you there, with Daphne, when I should be the one there with you."

"I feel like that, too. But I don't think I could bear it if you did come with her. The thought of you and Daphne sharing the bed you and I have shared so often...."

"Don't, my precious! Don't even think of it!"

"How can I help it? Oh, David!"

They sat in silence for a moment or two, until Wanda had recovered her composure. Then he said: "Look, sweetie, unless I take her and stay over the weekend, at least, Daphne won't go. But it will only be for three nights at the most that we'll both be there together, so why not put us in the two single rooms and you stay in your double bed?"

"Our bed, David."

"Yes, of course. Our bed. You stay in it."

"That's a wonderful idea if you're sure Daphne won't mind being separated from you."

"She'll be separated for the rest of the week—after I come

16

home. Even Daphne will see that it would be unreasonable for you to turn out of your room just to accommodate us for three nights."

As he finished speaking, the waitress arrived. As the girl served his vegetables, Wanda remarked: "Do you know, I've never known anybody eat broad beans in their pods before."

"Oh, yes, madame. When they are leetle."

"They're delicious," declared Bymeres. "I go for them whenever possible. But as Clara says, you can only get them young enough at this time of year, unless the frozen food people do them, of course. With parsley sauce they're really delightful. Try one! Clara, just put one on Mrs Mace's plate, please."

The Italian girl did as he asked and then stood back to watch as Wanda ate the bean. She was clearly delighted when Wanda described it as gorgeous.

"Thank you, Clara," said Bymeres. "Oh, the wine. Have you got it?"

"It is here, doctor."

When the girl had finally gone, David said, "Well now, about Daphne. Why don't you phone her and...."

"I've had an idea, David."

Again that little frown of annoyance at the interruption.

"What?" It was a curt monosyllable, emphasised as troublesome by him lifting his glass as though he couldn't afford to waste the time she might take in the telling of her idea.

"I know you'll think it ridiculous, but I still don't like the idea of you and Daphne coming together. I know I'd give myself away. I'd say something or do something to let the cat out of the bag."

He set the glass down. "You want to call it off?"

"I suppose I do, really. I should never have suggested it."

He was suddenly attentive and persuasive, reacting to her words almost with alarm. "Please don't do that, Wanda. It's a Good Samaritan gesture to Daphne, and a few days' break

17

from her will be wonderful for me, even if I'm not with you."

"I know, my pet. That's why I said I had an idea."

"Such as?"

"Couldn't you tell Daphne you will be free for the week-end so that she will agree to come, and then find at the last minute that you are on duty?"

He shook his head. "She'd dig her toes in at the last second of the eleventh hour. No, I'd have to bring her."

"Of course. Bring her and then be called back. Doctors can always arrange to be recalled unexpectedly, can't they?"

"Usually they don't have to arrange it. They can count on it happening."

"But to make sure—arrange an urgent call, at short notice. If I'm to put up with Daphne for ten days I at least want you to get some benefit from it, darling."

He grimaced. "Thanks." For a moment or two they ate in silence. Then he asked: "When shall I arrange to have the call made?"

"Couldn't it be as soon as you arrive at the cottage?"

"And have you greet me with it on the doorstep? Oh, no. If Daphne isn't unpacked and settled in, she'll just stay in the car and return with me."

"I suppose you're right. So make it after supper, David. After all, most urgent calls come at night, don't they?"

"Sad, but true."

Another little silence.

"How's your crab salad?"

"Absolutely delicious. How's your liver?"

"Magnificent. I love these little flabs of essence that congeal when the liver's fried. Over new potatoes they taste wonderful."

"And the beans? I must say I'd have thought a cheese sauce would have been more tasty."

"On no account must you use cheese." She felt it sounded like an instruction. But he expanded the statement by giving his reasons. If a cheese sauce were to be worthy of the name

18

in his eyes, it had to taste strongly of cheese. But a strong cheese taste would completely mask the delicate flavour of the tender young beans, so where was the sense in asking for such a delicacy, only to obliterate its palate-tickling savour with a far stronger but totally different taste?

She murmured agreement as she finished her salad. As he replenished her glass with the remains of the hock, he asked: "When are you going to give your invitation to Daphne? She might take a lot of persuading to accept it, you know."

"I'll manage it somehow. I'll phone her tonight."

"Look her up this afternoon. Go on from here to see her and make firm arrangements for next Friday. You'll achieve more in a face-to-face interview than you would over the phone."

She felt the arrangements were being taken out of her hands and felt a stab of resentment that he didn't think her capable of managing her own social affairs. But there seemed little point in refusing to agree to an eminently sensible tactic, even if it had been put to her more as an order than a suggestion.

"I take it you won't want to tell her I've seen you?"

"What do you think?" He glanced at his watch. "Time's pressing, poppet. Could we skip the sweet and order coffee straight away?"

"So you can get to your neonates and post-partums on time?"

"That's it, in essence. But it happens to be pre-natal this afternoon. Large, bulgy, fecund young women with all sorts of problems—mostly stemming from apprehension—but who are for the most part, incredibly cheerful. When they're pregnant, most of them are more friendly. I put it down to the fact that they feel safer in that state."

"Safer? Less likely to be chatted-up, you mean?"

"Something like that. But I think it goes deeper than that."

"I see. They wear pregnancy like a chastity belt. They think they are invulnerable, so they feel they can be matey."

He nodded and then raised his hand to attract the head-waiter's attention. When he had succeeded he mouthed the word 'coffee' and, satisfied that he had been understood, offered Wanda a cigarette.

Chapter 2

PILGRIM'S COTTAGE STOOD almost alone. Almost, because it had formerly been two cottages out of a row of three. The two had been made into one, and much to Wanda's regret, when the third had come on to the market, she had not been able to afford to buy. So she had near neighbours— a young couple with a child of three.

Both Daphne and David Bymeres were familiar with Pilgrim's. Wanda—a friend of both—had taken it six years earlier, after her divorce from Andrew Mace. Until Daphne had developed a serious chronic neurosis, both had been frequent visitors; but for the past eighteen months or two years, David had visited alone, even more frequently than before. Daphne, indrawn and withdrawn, had almost cut herself off from most of those who had been her friends. Now she had been persuaded to spend ten days with Wanda.

On the way down, David had attempted to entertain his unresponsive passenger by drawing her attention to all the old familiar landmarks, keeping up a running commentary much as a travel courier might do on a sight-seeing tour.

By the time they reached Long Munny village, he had been virtually exhausted.

"Here we are, Daphne. Long Munny. Remember the pub, the Four-Fingered Hand? Where we took Wanda and her mother for dinner that time? It's an old coach house. It got its name because the first landlord is said to have been born with only four fingers on each hand. As its name implies, it's a long village. Just a main street nearly a mile long. And the church? Hell of a great thing, built by a group of farmers and merchants who'd made enough money to name even the village after their most precious commodity. Munny! We've got to turn off soon to get to Wanda's. Remember?

She's out at Little Munny. You used to say it should be called Pin Munny. It's not really a village. Only a hamlet. No church, no pub. About sixteen houses all told, I suppose."

"Twenty-eight," Daphne had said surprisingly. "I counted them one day. Twenty-eight including the two new bungalows."

At that point David had turned right into the narrower looping road that ran to Little Munny and then on for a further mile to rejoin the main road at Flux corner. The side road, high-hedged and narrow, bisected Little Munny. At the top of the loop, on the right, the country opened out, and situated here were most of the original houses as well as the two new bungalows, the bricks of which showed up too red and the roofs too green in comparison with their neighbours. On the left, on the inside of the loop but set far back, were just three dwellings. Pilgrim's was in the middle, with its small attached neighbour on its left. On its right, but two broad gardens' widths away was a single small house of much later date than the cottages, with a seeming inability to grow old gracefully like its near companions.

Pilgrim's had a white, five-barred gate in its front hedge. This stood open, giving on to a track, rather than a drive, metalled with yellow-brown gravel. It was on the same level as the grass of the garden, and the edges were higgledy-piggledy where the two surfaces met. The way ran between and under large Blenheim apple-trees, past circular island gardens chock-full of bloom, and on to the patch of concrete in front of the new garage Wanda had built. This was at the end of the house, but separated from it by a twenty foot gap which would accommodate the oil lorry which came to fill the central heating tank at the rear and the local sewage tanker when it did its rounds to pump out the underground reservoir. Less than ten feet from the back of the cottage was a hedge, and after that, plough. The back door was at the end opposite the garage; the front door had been contrived and put under a small enclosed canopy so that it did not open—as once had been the case—straight into what was now Wanda's sitting room. This addition was the only feature that David did not wholly care for, but he recognised the necessity for it.

Their arrival had apparently cheered Daphne to the point where she asked for a conducted tour to view the alterations and improvements which had been carried out since her last visit. The staircase was new. When Wanda had moved in, just one of the former narrow flights was still left in place. But this had not suited her. Now a pleasant, wide flight in oak had been installed, rising from a corner of the dining room to run up to just outside the new bathroom. The old bathroom, fashioned from one of the original ground floor kitchens, was now converted into a cloakroom which, oddly, led off the sitting room. Upstairs, across the end of one of the single bedrooms, a false wall had been removed to reveal a space no bigger than a largish cupboard, separated by vertical beams from the main body of the room and just right for taking a very small, prettily upholstered settee that Wanda had found in a sale.

So now Pilgrim's was as Wanda had planned it. There was no downstairs hall. All the rooms led one from the other. If you entered by the back door, you found yourself in a large 'L' shaped kitchen, the bit out of the 'L' being occupied by a small laundry and pantry. The shorter stroke of the 'L' led directly, down a shallow step, through a wide doorless archway into the dining room. Opposite the archway was the door into the sitting room—a large, off-beat shape, with huge chimney and fire basket, and alcoves for such things as desk and bookcases. Altogether very satisfying for those who loved such dwellings, as Wanda obviously did.

It was almost seven o'clock when—all the first excitement over—David Bymeres joined his hostess in the sitting room.

"I've just been round the garden. God, I love this place of yours, Wanda. It's so absolutely just right."

"For the two of us, you mean?" She moved from the window where she had been rearranging a vase of flowers, and kissed him lightly on the cheek.

"That's just what I mean." He sat in an easy chair. "But I must say, Wanda, I wish you hadn't worn that dress."

23

"Why ever not?" She held the skirt in close and looked down at her legs. She was in lime green cotton, bare legs and sandals. "It's an old one I fished out...."

"Did you have to wear a mini skirt, tonight of all nights?"

"It's not a mini skirt. It's a bit shorter than present fashion dictates perhaps...."

"It nevertheless shows off a great deal of erotic thigh. I repeat, did you have to wear it? What are you trying to do? Torment the husband of your best friend?"

"I prefer to describe it as exciting my lover."

"You! You really have done it on purpose."

"I warned you the other day at lunch not to trust women or their motives."

He flung one leg over the arm of the chair and took cigarettes from his pocket. "So you did. No woman is an angel. And talking of angels, where's Daphne?"

"It's a bit late to ask that, isn't it? After the way you've been talking?"

He threw her a cigarette, which she caught expertly. "I came through all your rooms. She wasn't in any of them."

She used a table lighter. "It's not quite seven o'clock. So I'm not expecting her down just yet. She went up to unpack, and said she'd rest for an hour before coming down. I think she's fallen in love with that little bedroom and the settee and wants a bit of time on her own up there. Anyhow, I told her our dinner guests aren't due until half past."

"Ah, yes! Guests! I noticed you'd got the table set for six. All the silver, glass and napery out, and appetising smells in the kitchen."

"Oh, no! Not a smell of cooking! That's the one drawback to this house. I've got the extractor fan going, an air freshener doing its stuff, and I've left the door open."

"Don't worry. Nothing to notice. Just a good smell. Appetising."

"Could you tell what it was?"

"That was cooking? No. Tell me."

"It's to be a surprise for you."

"I like surprises. How about a drink? Sherry or gin?"

"Sherry, I think."

He got up and moved to a corner wine cupboard. As he poured the drinks, he said: "How did Daphne take the news that you're having dinner guests? She's not too partial to company, you know."

She moved to take the glass of sherry from him. "Steady on, there, you've slopped it on your suit."

He took out a still-folded handkerchief and mopped his front. "Damn! It will need to be cleaned again now."

"For those few drops?" She asked it humorously, but she guessed his vanity was showing again. The amount that had got on to his dark suiting would never show. "Go on, get your own drink."

He put the handkerchief away.

"Just as a matter of interest, David, why haven't you changed out of your suit and into slacks?"

"Have you forgotten? I'm expecting to be called back before bedtime."

"You're a rotten conspirator."

"How do you mean?" He sounded guilty.

"We know you're going back, but Daphne doesn't. For it to look genuine, that call should catch you unprepared—all dressed down for a weekend's break, not dressed up for business."

"You're right, of course. Ah, well, never mind! Cheers!"

"Cheers!"

He crossed over to the chair and sat down. She perched on the arm. He said: "Daphne isn't going to be the life and soul of your little party, you know."

She kissed his hand. "I know. So I've chosen my guests with care. Just three to make up the half dozen of us. They'll not worry her."

"Do I know them?"

"I don't think so. They could have seen you here of course...."

"Darling! One wrong word...."

"No, no. Mr and Mrs Enderby, an elderly couple who are very kind. He's a retired sweet manufacturer—perhaps that accounts for their sweet natures. They won't gossip. And Bill Spinnaker won't notice a thing. He's from one of those new bungalows, but his wife's in hospital expecting their first baby and believe me, he's so taken up with imminent parenthood that he'll not know what he's eating, let alone notice Daphne or you."

"Clever Wanda! But I assure you I'll notice what I'm eating. I hope you realise I skipped lunch in the rush to get down here."

"Poor darling! Never mind! It's all your favourite dishes so you'll be able to ..." The phone in the corner gave a preliminary tinkle and then started to ring properly. "... eat your fill and ... oh, damn that thing! Excuse me David." Her words were almost lost in the sound of the bell. She rose and crossed over to answer the call. "Mrs Mace, Pilgrim's Cottage."

The phone crackled a reply. She put her hand over the mouthpiece and turned to him. "Somebody wants to speak to Dr Bymeres urgently."

"Who?"

Into the phone. "Who is speaking, please."

"It's your Miss Hector from the surgery," she said, handing the instrument over to him. "It must be the call you arranged, but if so, it's hours early."

"I'll see what's happened." He paused a moment before saying, "Dr Bymeres here. What is it, Miss Hector?"

"I'm terribly sorry, doctor. I know you asked for a call at half past nine, but this is a real emergency."

"What is it?"

"Mr Cupwell of Stephen Street. He's apparently in great pain. His wife said you told her to call you at any time if...."

"Yes, yes I did. Look, Miss Hector, I've got my bag in my car. I'll go straight to Stephen Street from here. It's about ten miles, so I should make it in less than half an hour. Will you let Mrs Cupwell know that, please?"

"Of course, doctor. And I shall be here on duty until half past seven if you should want anything before then."

"Thank you, Miss Hector, I shouldn't need anything from the surgery. I'm on my way now." He put the phone down, turned towards Wanda and spread his hands. "The best laid schemes o' mice an' men.... Sorry, darling! This one's a true bill."

"You've really got to go?"

"Really! Just when you were telling me about how gorgeous the dinner is going to be." He walked across to her and kissed her on the nose. "I'll just whip upstairs and pick up my overnight bag. I'll not disturb Daphne."

"No. She'd want to go with you. Once you've gone she'll accept that she's stranded. Will you be back?"

"It won't be worth it, will it? I was going at half past nine anyway." He gulped the remains of his drink and looked up to see the disappointment on her face. "Look, I can't say. Don't keep dinner for me, but if I can get back for an hour, I will. In any case, I'll phone."

"That's all very well, David, but what if Daphne gets upset?"

"Pay no attention, my sweet. She'll enjoy her dinner. She always does. She eats hearty. After that she may play up a bit."

"Play up? You just said...."

"Oh, quite quietly. Usually she complains of a headache or some such thing. If she does that tonight, use it as an excuse for packing her straight off to bed. Then forget her. She'll be back to her usual depressing self in the morning. Now, that bag...."

He passed through into the dining room and up the stairs. Wanda crossed to the corner cupboard and poured herself another sherry. She gulped at it crossly. She had a feeling that the evening was going to be a disaster. With David to cope with Daphne, the party might just have been pleasant, but without him ... she muttered the word to herself: "Disaster".

When Bymeres came down again, she was waiting at the bottom of the stairs.

"Look, David, I think you'll have to come out here again tomorrow after all."

He released her hand. "Later, darling. I can't stop to talk now. We'll discuss it on the phone. Cheer up. I'll see everything turns out all right."

"For you, maybe."

His grin faded. "What do you mean by that?"

"Nothing. Off you go. There's somebody dying, isn't there?"

The cold consommé was a great success. A rather distrait Bill Spinnaker, a large, ungainly young man with a shock of fair hair, said he recognised the taste but couldn't quite place it. Old Mr Enderby, wearing a white alpaca jacket and an albert from his lapel buttonhole into his breast pocket, said that Wanda must be sure to give Mrs Enderby the recipe, while that good lady opined that one could tell as it went down that it was nourishing because of the wholesome taste. She claimed very gently to be a good judge, because at one time she had been a much-respected taster in her husband's confectionery business. Even Daphne went so far as to say that it was just the thing for a hot evening.

Wanda was delighted, but wondered how the rest of the menu would go down. She brought on game pâté, already served on little plates and a napkin of hot toast fingers. She asked Bill Spinnaker to serve the wine.

"Chianti, by crikey!"

"Don't you like it?"

"And how! First class plonk! Oh, I say, I didn't mean...."
He rescued himself from his embarrassment by adding: "I wonder if poor old Bella is getting anything like this in her maternity ward?"

"Hardly," said Daphne quietly. "It would ... well, it wouldn't be good for a baby, would it? It would ... what's the proper phrase? ... it would cross the placental barrier."

"But you'll have some, Mrs Bymeres?"

"Yes, please, Mr Spinnaker. I haven't had chianti for so long, and it reminds me of so many things. Do you remember, Wanda, when we were students, and we used to buy chianti

28

more because we liked the shape of the bottles and the straw covers than because we liked the wine?"

"But you do like it, don't you, Daphne?"

"Of course. I was trying to say that those things made choosing what wine to buy so much easier. It was nothing ... I merely...." She lapsed into silence, eyes down, shutting out the others. The thought occurred to Wanda that Daphne had just taken herself out of circulation, embarrassed by her own temerity.

"Everybody likes chianti," said Enderby, slipping into the breach manfully. "I suppose it's because so many of us go to Italy these days and sample it as the wine of the country. It is, as Mrs Bymeres says, so evocative. It brings back memories of happy times." He turned to his wife. "Do you remember the Casa Serena in Piano di Sorrento, my dear?" When his wife replied that she remembered very well, he launched into a story about buying a demijohn of chianti from a wine shop cut in the base of the cliff near Sorrento and dropping it when halfway up the steps from the harbour. The anecdote was long enough and pointless enough to allow Wanda the opportunity to clear the pâté plates and bring on the liver and bacon with its garnish of onions and mushrooms and the accompanying baby broad beans cooked in their pods and topped with parsley sauce.

Wanda now felt it safe to remark to her guests that this course had been prepared purely in honour of the absent guest. "David once told me he doted on liver and bacon and whole broad beans. I recalled him telling me when I saw the beans in the greengrocer's shop the other day. So I decided to surprise him."

"Very nice, too," said Mrs Enderby. "When I was a girl we always ate broad beans with white sauce. And my mother always cooked the little ones whole—recklings she called them—with boiled ham or bacon. They used to come out glistening, because the fat from the bacon used to coat them and make them very tasty indeed. But there, I've always loved bacon fat. There's nothing like it, is there, for frying eggs?"

29

Daphne looked up. "I didn't know David doted on liver and bacon. Oh, I knew he liked it, but no more than," she appeared to cast round in her mind, failed to find a comparison, and ended dully, "than anything else. Perhaps...."

"Yes?" said Wanda, trying to be a helpful hostess.

"Perhaps a wife becomes so used to feeding her husband that she forgets what he likes to eat most, because she concentrates too much on avoiding what he doesn't like and because she has to try and give him variety."

"That's very true, my dear," said Mrs Enderby. "What with avoiding things that will make our menfolk put on weight and remembering that in a three course meal you can't have two courses that are similar ... do you know what I did not long ago? I served curry for our main course and then dished up rice pudding to follow. George ate it, of course, but I was extremely worried about my mistake because I'd just read one of those prissy articles about women who dig early graves for their husbands with the help of the cooking utensils."

Daphne seemed to have forgotten David's likes and dislikes, and was concentrating more on her own. "Yes, please, Wanda. Yes, I like liver. I tend to eat a lot, you know. Or so David says. Some people like me do, you know. Try to eat their way out of worry, I mean." Such candour left Wanda aghast, but Enderby, again the diplomat, stepped into the breach.

"It doesn't show, Mrs Bymeres. If you'll forgive my saying so, there's not much of you. No excess weight. In the old days we'd have said you looked like two boards clapped together. But there, this slim fashion is all the rage these days, isn't it?"

Daphne actually smiled at him—just a little quirk of the lips. Wanda, anxious to keep the conversation going, and being unable to rely on Spinnaker, who was eating well—as though he hadn't had a square meal since his wife left for hospital—but was seemingly lost to his surroundings, turned to Mrs Enderby.

"You used the word reckling. It's not often used these days...."

"Same as runt," grunted Spinnaker, surprisingly. "Smallest and weakest animal in a litter."

"That's what I thought. An animal. But Mrs Enderby applied it to young beans, which are inanimate. Vegetable in fact."

Mrs Enderby laughed.

"My mother," she said, "was a country woman, and I dare say her vocabulary was not as sophisticated as perhaps would be the case today. So she used a word like reckling to describe anything small, animate or inanimate, knowing full well she would be understood. The little bun or biscuit that came at the end of a bake, for instance, made out of the scraps that remained, was a reckling to my mother. She always told us that we could have the recklings when she'd taken them from the oven. But in the case of broad beans, I would venture to suggest she wasn't so far out when she used the term, because we grew our own in those days, and we would never have cropped them when they were as small as this. That would have been uneconomic in our eyes. But when we actually did come to pick them, there were always some small ones—not old, stunted ones, but young, late starters. And those were the recklings—the little ones of the litter, if you like—which were separated out and cooked in their shells, much as we used to eat small peas in their shells just at that time of the season."

This explanation carried them almost through the main course, so that it was not long before Wanda was bringing on a lemon mousse.

"I make no apologies to anybody for this," she said with a laugh. "You're getting it because it's a favourite of mine, and I think it's a favourite of mine because I find it easy to make."

The mousse was in individual glasses, topped with cream, and decorated with a slice of lemon impaled on the rim. Wanda watched in anticipation as they tasted it. She used Kirsch in her recipe and enough beaten white of egg to

31

achieve a dreamlike consistency. She had come to expect approbation, and she got it.

From everybody except one person: Daphne.

"Wanda."

"Yes, Daphne?"

"Would you mind if ... I mean, I feel so very hot ... would you mind if I don't wait for coffee? I'm sure I've got a headache coming on, and...."

"My dear, go and sit down. Here, let me help you. We don't mind at all." Wanda realised she was talking for the sake of talking. The headache was no surprise because she had been warned about that, but its onset this early had taken her unawares. "Here, come through to the sitting room. The others will excuse you."

"No, please. I think I'll go up to my room and lie down. If ever I have attacks like this they go if I lie down and take my medicine."

Wanda took her arm as they reached the foot of the stairs in the corner of the dining room. "You look very flushed, Daphne. Are you sure you wouldn't like me to come up with you?"

"Perfectly sure. Please ... please don't bother about me."

"Shall I try to get in touch with David?"

"Oh, no. He'd only say I was playing my usual games. I'll be all right. Good night."

Wanda watched until Daphne rounded the bend in the stairs and then returned to the table.

"Migraine?" asked Enderby. "Or something that's disagreed with her?"

"I hope not, Mr Enderby."

"Of course not," said his wife. "It was a beautiful meal, and I for one feel no ill-effects. No, if you ask me, I think that young woman overeats just a little bit. You heard her earlier on. She thinks that if she doesn't put on weight it doesn't matter how much she eats. But she's wrong. She forgets that her stomach has to cope with it and that it could rebel at being overloaded."

32

"Mrs Bymeres is complaining of a headache, my dear, not a stomach ache."

She smiled at her husband. "Do you remember when John was little?" She turned to Wanda and said: "John is our son, you know." Then to her husband again. "When John was little and felt unwell he used to say he'd got a headache in his tummy. Well, my guess is that Mrs Bymeres has got a tummy ache in her head."

Spinnaker laughed. "I say, that's a jolly good way of explaining it, you know. I'll have to remember that for when my son...."

"Or daughter!" smiled Wanda.

"What? Oh, yes. Whichever it is. Anyhow, you know what I was going to say."

They moved to the sitting room for coffee. As she passed to and from the kitchen to fetch the percolator, Wanda listened at the bottom of the stairs. There was no sound from Daphne.

They were still chatting half an hour later when the phone rang. Spinnaker, who seemed momentarily to have forgotten the labour ward while he concentrated on Mrs Enderby's discourse on the best sweets to give to children, sprang from his seat like a grasshopper with an over-taut take-off mechanism. "That'll be for me. I gave them this number, I hope you don't mind, Wanda?" He was across the room and gabbling into the phone before Wanda was fairly on her feet. After a moment he disconsolately held the handset out to her. "It's Dr Bymeres for you."

"Hello, David."

"Wanda, I'm finished here, more or less. Is there any point in my coming down?"

"Not particularly. It's twenty past ten and the remains of supper are all cold and congealed."

"Right. I'll open a can here. How's Daphne?"

"She ate a hearty meal and then went off to bed with a headache."

"I warned you that was her usual form. Don't worry about her."

"But I am worried, David. It's all right for you. You're a doctor and know how to cope. But she looked very flushed to me."

"Don't worry, darling. If she wants anything, she'll ask for it. Otherwise, leave her alone and let her sleep it off. Sleep, you may recall, is the best doctor in the world. It cures more ills than we do."

"I suppose you're right. Will you ring again tomorrow?"

"Yes. I'm going to watch some cricket tomorrow afternoon, so it'll be evening before I ring."

"I'll tell Daphne. Goodbye, David. Enjoy the cricket."

"Was that Mrs Bymeres' husband?" asked Mrs Enderby. Wanda nodded.

"He's a doctor is he?"

"A very good one."

"And what has he to say about his wife's condition?"

"Tonight, you mean? Or generally?"

"Both."

"Well he doesn't treat her, of course. She has her own GP, and David never interferes. But he tells me Daphne is sometimes like this at nights and he just lets her sleep to get over it."

"Wise man. What is her complaint?"

"Nothing physical."

"She's a neurotic? I thought so. Long-term, I should say. So sad in a young woman. But it's the age we live in, my dear. Life today is conducted in a pressure cooker. The heat's put under us, we raise a head of steam and then blow our tops. Then we take drugs to pacify ourselves instead of turning the gas down to a level which would just about keep us on the move." The older woman shook her head. "We are so very foolish, my dear. So very foolish."

"I like that analogy," said Spinnaker. "But people won't play. Pressurise us long enough and we'll all turn into bone-meal soup. Most of us have lost our spines already."

"Nonsense," countered Enderby. "Now take you and your wife. If you have no belief in the future, what are you doing starting a family, may I ask?"

34

The chat went on. Just once, Wanda, who was listening out, thought she heard the sound of retching during a pause in the conversation. But the noise wasn't repeated so she did nothing about it.

Her guests left at midnight.

After their departure, she had a lot to do clearing up after them. She mustn't forget, she told herself, that she had Daphne as a staying guest for whom everything should be in apple-pie order in the morning. If it weren't, not only might Daphne feel she was unwanted, she might even feel constrained to help with the housework; and that would be no holiday for her, merely a change of sink.

So Wanda cleared away and washed up quietly, keeping an ear cocked for any sound from Daphne. After all had been put away and the cushions plumped up, she put out the lights and went upstairs. She looked at her watch. Almost one o'clock! She tiptoed along the little landing to listen at Daphne's door. No sound and no strip of light showing under the door. Satisfied, Wanda went to bed.

She was up at half past seven. Her best plan, she thought, was to spoil Daphne a little by taking her a breakfast tray. Orange juice, boiled egg, toast, marmalade, coffee ... she went outdoors and picked a small nosegay, adding it to the tray. It was five past eight when she carried it upstairs.

As she opened Daphne's bedroom door, forcing it open with her back once she had managed to turn the knob, Wanda grimaced with distaste. A sour smell of vomit assailed her. It raised a pang of apprehension in her mind. She tried to hurry in, banging the tray on the door jamb in the process. Once inside, she stood transfixed for a moment. Then she put the tray down slowly on the chest of drawers. Hesitatingly, she advanced towards the bed. Daphne had been violently ill. The vomit was a drying pool on the carpet beside the bed, with splashes up the bedside chest and the wallpaper. But even worse, Daphne herself. Wanda knew she was dead! Intuition? Or simply the curious stiff-necked position among the rumpled bedclothes? The trickle of congealed blood at the lower corner of the mouth?

Treading carefully, Wanda put out a hand to touch one peculiarly pale, uncovered foot. The feel of it burned her with cold. She looked again at the face. It was, she thought, faintly rimed with salt, and a moment or two passed before the explanation came to her. Daphne had sweated profusely, but had been incapable of wiping her own brow. The perspiration had dried on, leaving behind its spoor.

As she left the room, Wanda imagined she could discern the smell of sweat mingled with that of vomit now that much of the odour had escaped from the airless room.

As she went slowly downstairs, she also recalled the faint sound of retching she had heard the night before.

She again glanced at her watch. Not quite a quarter past eight. David should still be at home, even if he proposed going to the surgery on a Saturday morning. She dialled and waited impatiently for him to answer. She found cigarettes and a lighter in her housecoat pocket and managed, single handed, to light up.

"Dr Bymeres."

It was his professional voice. The one he reserved for patients. She was accustomed to it, and had never previously thought of it as anything else but funny. This morning it irritated her. It sounded competent enough, but smug and autocratic, pitched to ensure that no patient should ever imagine that Dr Bymeres was not in complete command of the clinical situation.

"David, it's Wanda."

"Wanda! How nice! But what on earth ... ?"

"It's Daphne."

"What is?"

"She's dead, David."

"Dead? You're sure?"

"Positive. I went in with her breakfast tray and found her. She's cold ... and stiff, and there's vomit and ... David, it's horrible." The hysteria had been delayed, but now it was mounting. She could feel it surging through her mind, taking charge as she fought to stop it engulfing her.

"Steady, Wanda, steady." Now his voice had an edge to

36

it. It helped her mind to focus, helped to prevent her just going over the top of reason.

"You must come, David. Hurry, please."

"Of course I'm coming. But if she's dead I must inform Ruloph Spiller...."

"*If* she's dead? She *is* dead, David."

"I meant *as* she's dead, Wanda."

"And who's this Rudolph Spiller?"

"Daphne's doctor. I haven't treated her. Can't treat her. So we've got to get Spiller. He's the only one who can sign the certificate and it's a hundred to one he'll want to examine her."

"Well, please hurry."

"Leave it to me, Wanda. You sit down and have some strong coffee. I'll be there in less than half an hour."

The phone went dead. She put the handset down and went through to the kitchen. The percolator was still hot. She drank the coffee black, and then went upstairs to finish dressing. She guessed there was going to be a lot of coming and going, and she had better be prepared for it.

She was brushing her hair when the thought struck her. She rushed downstairs and phoned the Enderbys. Yes, they informed her, they were perfectly well. Why? Mrs Bymeres was ill? No, they were not surprised that Mrs Bymeres was not too well this morning. They'd hinted as much last night. Spinnaker, too, was nervously fit. He was so anxious for Wanda to get off the phone in case a call came from the hospital that he neglected to enquire why she had asked.

Slowly she walked to the back door and into the garden. She didn't simply want to wait for David indoors. She wanted to get the stench of vomit and sweat and death out of her nostrils.

Chapter 3

DETECTIVE SUPERINTENDENT George Masters was on weekend duty at the Yard. Though he was keener than most on his job, he still loathed being cooped up in an office on a Sunday afternoon, particularly on a hot summer's day. This part of London stood down at weekends. He always had the depressing feeling that it was dead. He liked to look out and see the people and bustle of the workaday world, otherwise he felt isolated and hard done by. At the slightest excuse, he would find a reason for getting out and about. He called it using his initiative in carrying out his duties fully and correctly, but privately he knew that many of the little incidents he went to see for himself could quite adequately be dealt with by the junior officers on the spot.

One of his great assets was his ability to cope with paper work quickly; where so many of his colleagues sighed with resignation as soon as they took a pen in their hands, and then proceeded to stumble slowly and unwillingly through whatever bumf was on their desks, he could whip through at speed. It left him with more unoccupied time on his hands than most, and permitted him to do a fair amount of professional reading which, among his less academic colleagues, was a bore equal to that of writing reports. But it helped Masters to be the complete copper that most regarded him as. But the complete detective is—like the complete soldier—a practical man, not simply a chair polisher or, if such a phrase is too pejorative, an administrative wizard who knows what should and must be done but is incapable of putting it into practice himself.

On this particular Sunday afternoon he had quickly tired of reading. From the dearth of phone calls, he guessed that London was having a post-lunch siesta. The weather was too hot for instant crime. Probably after night fall....

His reverie was interrupted by a knock on the door and Detective Inspector Green came in. Green was only about two years from retirement. He and Masters had worked together a lot in the past few years, but they had never seen eye to eye within the team. When the party had been under pressure from outside, Green had rallied round and lent support, but only because he was a policeman first, last and always and wouldn't willingly allow anybody to knock the force even when it was represented by Masters. The two men were opposites in every way. Masters a young flier; Green an ageing subordinate. Masters a dresser; Green slovenly. Masters brilliant; Green a plodder. Masters to the right of centre politically; Green a rabid left-winger. And though these difficulties need have been of no account had the two not been antipathetic, they were, in fact, a source of such constant irritation that both men had frequently sought to end the association: Green by constant written applications for a transfer; Masters by verbal requests for a rejigging of his team. All had been ignored on the simple grounds that the team had been successful, and nobody in his right mind breaks up a winning team. But now things were different. Sergeant Brant, nominally Green's right hand man, had just been married and promoted to a new official security job. When this had happened, it had been decided that as a new sergeant would be required in Masters' murder squad, he may as well be one who could come over with the DI with whom he usually worked, who could replace Green. Anderson had pronounced on Thursday. The arrangements would be put in hand forthwith.

Green stopped awkwardly just inside the door and fished out a crumpled packet of Kensitas.

"Mind if I smoke?"

"Go ahead." Masters was watching him from his big desk chair. Green always bought heavy suits and footwear. Too heavy for weather like this. The trousers were unpressed and the jacket powdered with ash. Green advanced to put the dead match in the ashtray.

"I didn't know you were on duty today," said Masters. "You're not on my list."

"I've been to see Anderson."

"This afternoon?"

"This morning. He was in late on, before lunch. We've had a drink together."

"I see. I suppose he told you the old firm is to be broken up and you're going out to one of the Divisions as you asked."

"He told me that on Thursday. Can I sit down?"

"Help yourself. Yes, he spoke to me on Thursday, too."

"It appears nobody's got a place for me," said Green. Masters wasn't surprised. Most of the Divisional hierarchies knew Green and were aware of his limitations and character. None would be willing to fill an important post with such a man.

"So what is to happen?"

"I know there are holes for DI's in at least two Divisions."

Masters had no choice but to ask: "You think they've refused to have you?"

Green nodded.

"I'm not surprised," said Masters. "They'll want to get somebody who's got quite a few years to go yet. You'd no sooner be settled in than somebody else would have to get used to the patch." It was a good lie, and Masters was pleased with it. At least he hadn't needed to tell Green that nobody wanted him. Full stop.

"You reckon that's the reason?"

"I can't think of any other. You've got a good track record. You and I together have done our stuff as well as anybody and better than most, although I say it as shouldn't."

"Hmm!"

"You question that?"

"No. But where's the credit gone?"

"Largely to me," admitted Masters. "Just as failure would have been blamed on me."

"Would you be prepared to ring up the two Divisions and ask them to take me?"

"No. I'm not going to interfere in their business. I should object if somebody tried to make me alter a decision which I'd taken after full consideration of all the facts involved."

"Thanks. Do you know who they both want?"

"No idea. Who?"

"Hill."

Sergeant Hill had been with Masters for some years. He was long overdue for promotion, but here again Authority had held its hand—at the expense of the individual—in order not to break up the winning team. The news that Hill was now being sought as a DDI was good to hear. Masters had asked that the sergeant should be promoted on countless occasions, with no success. Now it appeared there was some hope that Hill would get what he thoroughly deserved.

"That's shaken you, has it?" asked Green with a smirk, wrongly construing Masters' silence as dismay or discomfiture at the prospect of losing another able member of his team.

"I'm delighted—if Hill is really going to be made up."

"He is. Anderson said so."

"He deserves to be. And one other thing."

"What's that?"

"If two Divisions have asked for him it means that not all the honour and glory sticks to me. Some of it rubs off on to you others apparently."

"Not enough to help me."

"You're not going to be unemployed, you know."

"Mebbe not. But look at the jobs I'll get given. The dregs."

"A couple of years' not too arduous work."

"That's what you think! It's the dregs that take the leg work—at all hours of the day and night."

"What have you ... ?" The internal phone rang on Masters' desk. He forgot what he was asking and picked up the handset. He listened for the best part of a minute, keeping the earpiece close to his ear so that the message wouldn't spill out to Green, who was not above listening consciously if the opportunity arose.

"Right, Chauncy, I'll come along straight away."

He put the phone down.

"Would you wait here."

"A job?"

"An outside one. Commander C's duty deputy."

"I heard. There's only one Chauncy White I know of round here."

"Commander C says you're to take it," said White. "The North Downs Area mob are scared stiff of it."

"Why?"

"Because the doctors won't sign the certificate. Either of 'em. Her own GP or the police surgeon. But she's a doctor's wife. And you know that the first person they look at is the husband."

"This Dr Bymeres?"

"That's the one. But he wasn't present, although they reckon it's a doctor's crime. So they can't tie it up, and they've an understandable reluctance to arrest the wrong person—particularly a doctor."

"Why particularly?"

"The medical aspect makes 'em shudder. So they want to unload. They've asked for us, and the commander says if it's up anybody's street, it's up yours."

Masters nodded. "I haven't got a full team. In fact, if Hill is going, I shall be alone."

"Hill going? Oh, yes, but we can hold that up for a day or two."

"Green's been told he's no longer with me, and I haven't got either his replacement or Brant's."

"Oh, hell!"

"If it's all right with you, Chauncy, I'll take Green—if you can square it with Anderson."

"No squaring needed. Green's gone into the Pool. I can draw on it at my discretion."

"Right. That'll have to do me. Green and Hill. The three of us."

"Sure? I can get you a buckshee sergeant—or failing that a DC."

"Don't worry, judging by what you've told me, I shan't have to set up an Incidents Room, thank heaven. I can't envisage much house-to-house work or beating waste ground."

"No-o. I should think it'll be pure detection. Right up your alley. I'll get in touch with Green and warn him."

"Don't worry. He's in my office."

Sergeant Hill was driving. Masters was sitting beside him. Green—pathetically unsure of himself in traffic—sat on the nearside rear seat.

"You've not told me anything about this job except which way to drive, chief. What is it? Murder?"

Masters was loading his pipe with Warlock Flake. He spent a second or two sucking at it to make sure it would draw well before replying.

"So far, it can only be called a suspicious death."

Green asked: "You mean they haven't established murder?"

Masters was lighting his pipe. Hill, driving south westwards was squinting into the afternoon sun and negotiating heavy weekend traffic. But he found time to reply to the DI.

"How does one establish murder, exactly?"

"Don't let impending promotion make you cocky," sneered Green.

"It's a valid question, nevertheless," said Masters. "This woman, Mrs Daphne Bymeres, was a chronic neurotic but physically she was as fit as any other woman in her early thirties. Yet she went and died in the night."

"What from?"

"Basically from cerebral haemorrhage and a massive heart attack."

Green sucked a tooth. "Could happen to anybody at any time. That's natural causes."

"Ah, yes. But if a skilful doctor has had you under his eye regularly for the past eighteen months, and has recently examined you thoroughly, without finding the slightest hint of predisposing causes, what then?"

"It wouldn't be the first time a quack has made a mistake."

"Agreed. But when the police surgeon agrees with the GP that the certificate should not be signed without a pathologist's report, what then?"

Green offered a crumpled pack of Kensitas over the seat so that Hill could reach it. "Have we had the pathologist's report yet?"

"Not officially. But he said enough off the record to make the North Downs Area Constabulary pretty sure that natural causes was not the answer."

"So they panicked and sent for us. Usual form. Everybody sends for us when they're on a hiding to nothing. They never give us first bite at the cherry so that we can draw an easy one now and then. When did it happen?"

"She went to bed after dinner on Friday night and was found dead in bed next morning."

Green grunted. "It stands out a mile."

"What does?"

"She was poisoned. I bet she puked all over the place and then snuffed it."

"Oddly enough, she did as you've described, but there's been no toxic substance found in her vomit or her body, except for traces of the medicine she was taking for her condition."

"Overdose?" asked Hill.

"The report says not."

"But the locals want to treat it as murder."

"Wouldn't you?" asked Green, switching his stand. "A chronic neurotic—she's an obvious candidate for murder. A young doctor with a wreck of a wife, with his hormones getting restive, would want to be rid."

"There is such a process as divorce," said Hill drily.

"It's not fast enough, chum. Two years, three years, five years. The law's delays."

"Hold it, a moment," said Masters. "I've tried to impress upon you that we'll have to satisfy ourselves there has been foul play before we even have a problem to solve. As the DI has said, on the face of it, intracranial haemorrhage and acute cardiac failure are natural causes, usually. We'll have to decide whether or not these were induced unnaturally before we look for who could have induced them."

"The doctors aren't satisfied."

"True enough. And neither should they be. The one treating Mrs Bymeres for severe depression has to decide whether he'll agree he was incompetent in not foreseeing this if it was a natural death, or he's got to suggest it was unnatural. He must take the second course, mustn't he? So he refuses a death certificate. Then along comes the police surgeon who's never seen the woman before in his life. Her own doctor has refused a certificate. Can he sign one? It's not likely, is it?"

Green grunted approval of this logic. Masters continued. "Now, as an investigating officer, with two doctors ganging up on you, what would your reaction be?"

"I'd do what the locals have done," said Hill. "I'd scream for help. If it is murder it's likely to be a bastard to solve, if it isn't—well, there's no harm been done."

"There's enthusiasm for you," said Green. "Where are we going?"

"Little Munny."

"I asked for our destination, not the state of your bank balance."

Masters didn't rise to Green's wit, though he was pleased to hear it in his taciturn assistant. He spelt the name of the hamlet and then added that they were heading for Pilgrim's Cottage.

"A happy band," said Green, unlike his usual self. Masters could only assume that the DI was cheerful at sharing at least one last case with his erstwhile companions. Hill concentrated on his driving and was soon nearing Long Munny.

"Are we staying down here, chief?"

"We'll see whether the locals have booked us in anywhere."

"I was just going to say that the pub—the Four-Fingered

Hand—looked okay if we are. Turn right here? Ah, yes. Little Munny one mile."

"Half a mo'," said Green, who seemed happier still now they were off the main road. "This bit of capurtle who died, did she live at this Pilgrim's Cottage?"

"She was down here for a stay in the country. The house belongs to a friend of hers, Mrs Wanda Mace."

"And where does Mr Mace come into all this?"

"There isn't one. Or, at least, not visible. She's a divorcee."

"So the two women were alone in the house last night! I can see possibilities here."

Masters made no comment. He was looking out for the first signs of Little Munny. Hill was concerned with keeping his eyes open for places where it would be possible to pass, should another car come in the opposite direction down the little road. At last Little Munny opened out, and Hill saw the Panda and another car parked near the name board of Pilgrim's Cottage. He turned in.

"Police cars at the gate, mini in the garage," said Green, "and yellow Renault parked at the door."

As Hill stopped close to the open garage doors, a constable in uniform came from the back door of the cottage. He was in shirt-sleeve order, young and alert.

"Good afternoon, constable. My name is Masters. You're expecting me."

"Afternoon, sir. Yes. I was told to keep an eye out for you. The DI's inside, sir. In the kitchen."

"He's the only one here other than you?"

"We're expecting the police surgeon between half past four and five, sir. The DI thought you would want to talk to him."

"Then whose is the yellow Renault?"

"Oh, that's Dr Bymeres', sir. He's inside with Mrs Mace."

"Hey, matey," said Green, climbing out of the car. "Have you ever seen that yellow Renault before this weekend?"

"Often, sir. I've seen it parked many a time just where it is now, and in Munny a few times."

"So the doctor and his missus were frequent visitors here?"

The constable pushed his flat hat back from his brow and stepped aside as Masters opened his door. "Well now, sir, as to Mrs Bymeres—that's the deceased, you know—ever being here, I can't say. But the doctor himself, yes. Of course, I didn't know he was a doctor, not until yesterday, nor did I know he was married. The talk in the village was just that he was Mrs Mace's man-friend, like, she being a divorced woman but still young and good-looking." As Green continued to stare at him, the constable finished apologetically: "It seemed the natural conclusion for folks to come to."

Green nodded. "Of course. Thanks, matey. You've been a great help."

"We might as well go inside and see what we can learn," said Masters.

"This way, sir."

"DI Wrotham," said the man sitting at the kitchen table. The pale blue washable top was littered with paper. His jacket hung over one chair-back; a packet of cigarettes, a box of matches and an ashtray were on another.

Masters introduced the three of them and looked round. There was a nice blend of the old and the new here. The kitchen was big, with all the latest gadgetry around. Eye-level cooker, fridge, freezer, electric mixer and blender, ironing board that folded up into the wall, breakfast bar with two blue-topped stools in addition to the table and chairs.

"How about a cup of chai, constable?" Green was a tea addict, but steadfastly refused to call it char. His wartime experience in the desert had indelibly seared on his mind the Arabic form rather than the Indian. It caused him to be misunderstood on occasion. He had to translate for the constable now. "Tea, laddie, tea. Strong tea."

"You'll have heard something of the problem," said Wrotham. "But if there's anything else I can tell you . . . ?"

"I understand we shall get the medical picture quite soon from the police surgeon." Masters sat on one of the chairs. It looked too frail and small for his weight and size, but it stood up to the load manfully.

47

"I asked Doc Theddlethorpe to come in specially when I was told you were on your way. He'll be better at it than me. I can never get all these medical things right. He was talking about intracranial haemorrhage and I thought it was *inter*cranial. So he started explaining and before I knew where I was I was being lectured on supranational something or other which had nothing whatever to do with the case. As if the job wasn't difficult enough in everyday language!"

"Cheer up," said Green. "We like that sort of thing—and I don't think!" He took a chair at the end of the table. "But apart from the jargon, what've you got? Turning out juicy, is it?"

Wrotham looked slightly bewildered.

"Juicy?"

"The motive, chum? Lust, for instance?"

"I don't see how it can be. I mean, her husband wasn't here."

"Maybe he wasn't, but my spies tell me her hubby was more than a bit friendly with Mrs Mace."

"You mean you think Mrs Mace could have killed her, here in her own house? Bit obvious, isn't it?"

"I've known obviouser," replied Green. "Ah!" He sighed deeply as the constable placed a large blue and white banded mug of steaming tea in front of him. "Just what the doctor ordered, and if everybody stuck to just what the doctor ordered, we shouldn't have games like this to play on a Sunday afternoon."

Masters accepted his tea. Hill took his standing up. He said: "It sounds as if you think Dr Bymeres has a perfect alibi because he wasn't here overnight."

"I didn't say that. But he brought his wife down, intending to stay over the weekend. He was suddenly called back early on Friday evening, before the dinner party Mrs Mace was giving for him and his wife. I've checked at his surgery that the call was both genuine and unexpected, so he couldn't have known about it in advance. His wife was in her room when he left, and she was perfectly okay at dinner time. She went to bed with a headache after dinner. Saturday morning

48

she was found dead. And she wasn't poisoned or ... or injured in any way. So I don't see how we can make a case out against Bymeres. Not yet, anyway."

Masters stirred his tea. "But we mustn't forget that for some killings, alibis for the time of death are meaningless."

"I know that, sir. For instance, say I see you in a pub at six o'clock and leave at half past. I don't see you again that night and I can prove I don't. But that's no alibi if I've slipped something in your drink and you die at ten o'clock. My alibi's no earthly. But this isn't a poison case."

"Quite. But the same could apply to death by explosives or time-switched electrocution for instance. Or any one of a number of ways of delayed-action killing, I suspect."

Wrotham ran his hand through his hair. "That's fine, sir, if you can find out how it was engineered as a delayed-action killing. There aren't any fractured gas pipes or anything of that sort here, and the woman died of intracranial haemorrhage and heart failure."

"Everybody who's murdered dies of some such thing," said Green. "You talk of somebody being electrocuted, but what does he really die of?"

"Heart failure, I suppose."

"And somebody who's been coshed over the head?"

Wrotham shrugged. "I know. Brain haemorrhage or some such. But I still think that in those cases it's easy to see what caused the damage, whereas here we can't. Or I can't. You might be able to sort it out."

"We'll try," said Masters pacifically. "Now is there anything more you feel you ought to tell us?"

"Not really. But you'll be able to get me at HQ if you want me. Constable Hampton here," he nodded towards the constable who was taking his tea at the draining board, "he lives in Long Munny, so you can get him easily if you want any local information. And he's booked you in tentatively at the Four-Fingered Hand. If you want the rooms, he's got to confirm them before five."

"That's kind of you. Yes, we'll take them, constable."

"Right, sir. I'll go down there. I can't ring up very easily

49

from here, because the phone's in the sitting room and Mrs Mace is in there with Dr Bymeres."

"Fine. Go when you like."

"I'll go, too," said Wrotham. "That's if you don't mind. I've been running around like a scalded cockerel since nine o'clock yesterday morning."

Masters smiled his acquiescence. Constable Hampton was rinsing his cup at the sink under the window. "I say, sir, it looks as if Dr Bymeres is leaving."

"Then stop him. Superintendent Masters will want to talk to him."

"No, no," said Masters. "Let him go. By the time we've spoken to Mrs Mace and Dr Theddlethorpe it'll be enough for today. We can find him easily enough when we want him."

They heard the murmur of goodbyes, the car door slam, and the noises of engine and tyres on gravel.

"That's him away," said Hill.

"And us," said Wrotham. "Well, sir, the best of luck. He was gathering his papers as he spoke. "We've all heard about your successes in the past. . . ." He turned to Green: "And yours, Mr Green. Got a name up in the force for having a memory better than the central computer, you have. So we'll hope this one turns out like the others."

Wrotham and Hampton left by the kitchen door.

"Nice chap, that," said Green, plainly pleased that his name should be a byword in the provincial forces. "Very nice chap. Not much of a jack for this sort of case, perhaps, but at least he recognises his limitations. He's probably very good with routine rural crime and organising foot-and-mouth disease precautions."

Hill tossed him a cigarette. "Come off it."

"Ta! What d'you mean, come off it?"

"He'd butter anybody up to be shot of this lot."

"And what do you think you'll do as a DI when it gets tricky?"

"Ask for help, of course. Even from you, maybe. But I'll stay with it myself. Not give up and hand over."

50

"We'll see."

"Cut it out, you two," said Masters. "Now, first off let's see what we've got. Despite Wrotham's belief to the contrary, it is possible...."

He left the sentence unfinished. They had all heard the sitting-room door open. Through the wide archway which led from the kitchen he could see the woman who crossed the dining room, rounding the end of the table gracefully and almost leaping the little step up to the kitchen.

Wanda Mace, he thought, looked wonderful. He got the impression she was a little pale under the tan. But there was, as far as he could see, no other indication that there had so recently been a tragedy in the cottage. She was in a pale blue summer dress, with bare arms and legs. The belt was broad, with a big metal buckle: the only relief from the blue. Even her little shoes were blue. Her eyes were neither wary nor troubled as was so often the case in women unexpectedly thrown into contact with sudden death and police enquiries. As he got to his feet to greet her, Masters found himself approving not only of her appearance, but also of her bearing and attitude.

"Good afternoon, ma'am. Mrs Mace?"

"Yes, I'm Wanda Mace. Are you the gentlemen from Scotland Yard?"

Masters did the introductions.

"I saw your car arrive. David—that's Dr Bymeres—and I waited because he thought you might like to talk to him. But as you didn't come in, he decided to go."

Her voice was low pitched and pleasant. Green was obviously impressed. He went so far as to stub out the cigarette Hill had given him, and then to offer a new packet of Kensitas to Wanda.

"I'd love one. But couldn't we smoke it in the sitting room. I could make you some tea, too."

"We've had some, thank you, but we would like to talk," said Masters. "If now is a convenient time for you ... but perhaps you'd like tea yourself."

"I've had some, too. David said he was parched." She

51

turned and led the way to the sitting room.

As they took seats, Masters said: "So you were expecting us, Mrs Mace?"

She was sitting in a little nursing chair: a gem of a piece, probably of some antiquity. She looked wonderful, he thought, on the low seat. It had no arms, but a back high enough to frame her almost white hair. He, himself, had selected a brown hide club chair beside the fireplace and almost opposite her. Green had the sofa, which ran out at right angles from the chimney breast. Hill had a tapestry chair, all curly wood and sage greens in the upholstery. Masters noted how everything was subdued in here. The window faced east. By this time of day the sun had gone from that side of the house. It would reappear later, just before setting, in the little window on the other side of the room: a little window no bigger than one to be found in a bathroom, squeezed into its place by the cloakroom which led off this same wall of the sitting room.

Subdued. The oak beams, the slightly grimy bricks of the fireplace, the sage green and dark tan of the furniture, a carpet as brown as burgundy with a grey medallion pattern, the many-coloured but far from garish curtain of books in an alcove. A piece of silver here and there, and the twinkle of cut glass from a minute rose bowl and a taller vase. A few small pieces of porcelain bric-à-brac that needed to be studied at close range before their colours shouted their presence. And the absence of direct sunlight. A cool, subdued, low-ceilinged room of beauty, promising gracious living and a snugness in winter that even in June made one long for the dark nights with closed curtains and the howl of a gale so that one could experience it fully.

"I was told by Mr Wrotham that you were coming, but I cannot understand why Scotland Yard of all people should be implicated in this ..., this nightmare."

"Just because it is a nightmare ma'am," said Green surprisingly. "Nightmares are frightening things at any time. Those that happen when you're awake, rob you of sleep. But if they can be explained rationally they lose their power to disturb you. And that's what we're here for. To see if we can't get rid of this one."

She stared at him for a moment as though trying to understand his words. He grinned at her, slightly self-consciously but nonetheless reassuringly. "I still don't see why you're here. There has been an unexpected death which must be satisfactorily explained, but no crime has been committed." The little frown of puzzlement on her brow seemed to denote genuine bewilderment and gave all three men the impression that she was speaking the truth.

"Mrs Mace," said Masters gently, "you must be aware that neither Mrs Bymeres' own doctor...."

"Dr Spiller."

"Spiller? I didn't know his name. Neither Dr Spiller nor Dr Theddlethorpe, the police surgeon, felt able to sign a death certificate for Mrs Bymeres. She was a young, healthy woman in whom intracranial haemorrhage and massive cardiac trouble could not be expected. Unless such trouble is foreseen, it must be explained before a death certificate can be issued. By either doctor. This means that somebody must seek the explanation by digging deeper into the mystery. The people called upon to do such digging are the police and the forensic services, Mrs Mace. In the case of Mrs Bymeres, the local police realised that perhaps they are less able to cope satisfactorily with an investigation which has medical overtones than we are at the Yard. So we have been asked to sort the matter out."

"Sort it out? Treat it as murder, you mean?"

"No. I didn't say that, nor did I intend to imply it."

"What then?"

"We propose to treat it as a mysterious death—which is exactly what it is. You can't explain it, the doctors can't as yet, nor the local police. But the explanation must be found— for everybody's sake—and that is our task. Only if we subsequently suspect that there has been foul play, which is what I suspect you mean when you say no crime has been committed, will we begin to treat Mrs Bymeres' death as a case of murder."

"I see."

"And, incidentally, I should like to say at the outset, how very sorry we all are about Mrs Bymeres' death."

"Thank you."

"Now, if we could have a chat, Mrs Mace, we can begin to get this affair sorted out."

Chapter 4

MASTERS ASKED FOR an account of what had happened at Pilgrim's Cottage on Friday evening. "With as much detail as possible, please," he added.

"I'd better begin," said Wanda, "at the time Daphne and David arrived."

"Which was when?"

"A little before half past four. I had a tea tray waiting, but it was some time since Daphne had been here, and I'd been having a few alterations made, and she insisted on seeing them first. So I showed her round, pointing everything out and trying to be as bright and cheerful as possible because she was a chronic depressive, you know, and pretty morose. It was quite hard work trying to get and keep her interest. But I managed it somehow. The little bedroom where she died helped."

"The room did? Did she like it that much?"

"It's a sweet little room, and we'd discovered a false wall which, when knocked down, gave us just a bit of extra space. Just a couple of square yards, but it was separated from the rest of the room by three or four upright beams and a few cross timbers. We removed some of these cross ones to make a sort of doorway between the uprights, but the rest were left in place and I was able to decorate the little alcove with a nice rug, a very small sofa and wall lights. This seemed to delight Daphne, and when she heard that she was to sleep there she was quite excited.

"During this time, David had been bringing in the bags from the car, and he put hers in there, opened up her vanity case and put her things on the dressing table. He put his own stuff in the other single room and I finally got Daphne down here. I left David showing her the new cloakroom just off here," Wanda stopped, and pointed to the old plank door behind Masters, "and I put the kettle on for tea.

"We had tea in here. There was a sponge cake. Daphne and David both had a piece. Then we sat and chatted until about a quarter to six. The clock chimes the quarters, as you've probably heard. It was my signal to be up and doing. I had invited another three guests to join us for dinner, and though it was mostly a cold meal and nearly all ready, I still had a few things to do, including laying the table.

"Daphne insisted on helping me to wash up the tea dishes. There weren't enough of them to worry about, but I let her as she seemed to want to, and we left David in here looking at a magazine. After we'd washed up, Daphne said she'd like to go up to her room. I was very pleased and asked her if she would bathe before she had her rest, as that would leave the bathroom free for me and for David later. I told her I wasn't expecting our guests before half past seven and she said she would be down at that time.

"David must have gone into the garden through the front door here. At any rate, I didn't see him as I laid the table. I put the main course in the oven and then went upstairs to bathe and change. I got down here about ten to seven and David joined me from the garden. We helped ourselves to drinks, and while we were chatting, the phone rang—about seven o'clock, it was—and David was called back to attend to a patient who was in a bad way. He hadn't unpacked, so in case he couldn't get back on Friday night, he took his bag with him.

"I had one or two last minute things to do, like putting the vegetables on, and I did those after David went. I'd just about finished when Daphne came down and our other guests arrived. We all had a drink in here, then went through to eat about ten to eight. We had a simple four course meal and coffee, a couple of bottles of wine and a lot of chat. Daphne ate a hearty meal—and I mean hearty—and enjoyed her wine. Then when we were getting up from the table, about half past nine, she missed the coffee—said she had a headache and would go to bed. David told me that she often got headaches like this, and I wasn't to worry, but I offered to go up with her. She said she preferred to go alone, and the people at the dinner table said they weren't really surprised at her having a headache because she'd eaten so much for a small, slim woman. I remember somebody spoke of some child who overate talking about having a headache in his tummy.

"Anyhow, that was that. The four of us who were left came in here. David rang sometime later to say he had finished but he would stay at home and get something to eat. Nobody heard anything of Daphne. At least, I thought once I heard a faint sound of retching, but it stopped, so I thought I had been mistaken. The party broke up at midnight. I then had an hour's work clearing away and washing up, so it wasn't till after one that I went upstairs. I listened at Daphne's door. There was no sound and no light was showing under the door, so I assumed she was asleep. The last thing I wanted was to disturb her, so I went to bed. Yesterday morning at eight o'clock I took her up a breakfast tray. When I went into the room I smelt and saw that she had vomited. When I put the tray down and took a closer look at her, I saw she was dead, but I touched her foot to make sure. She was stone cold. So I came down here and rang David. I caught him at home. He rang Dr Spiller and then came on here. Dr Spiller arrived, and after seeing Daphne, rang the police."

Masters nodded as if approving of the way she had told her story. Then, as he filled his pipe, he started to ask questions.

"Mrs Mace, you said that Mrs Bymeres had not seen the alterations because she had not been to the cottage for some time. How long?"

"Almost two years, I think."

"Ever since she became a chronic neurotic, in fact?"

"Yes."

"Yet I am informed that Dr Bymeres is a frequent visitor here. His car has often been seen in your drive and in the village."

"That's right. I often see David. Sometimes twice a week when he can get away."

"Would you mind telling me the nature of the relationship between you and Dr Bymeres?"

She didn't hesitate. "We are lovers. I suppose you would describe me as David's mistress."

Masters silently thanked heavens for modern morals and candour. "A doctor's mistress?"

"I am not his patient. There is no professional misdemeanour on his part."

"I see that, and doctors are human. But you'll forgive me if I mention that I find it strange for a man's mistress to invite his wife—as a house guest."

"I suppose it is a little out of the ordinary." She helped herself to a cigarette from the box on the low table. "But Daphne and I are old friends. We were, at one time, great friends. What girls call 'best friends'." Green gave her a light. She smiled her thanks. "I knew her before she knew David. We went up to university together. In our second year we managed to get into a hall of residence. David was already there—a fourth year medical student. Daphne and I were together the first time she met David. Anyhow, she married him after his time in hospital, and by that time I'd married Alex.

"We all four remained good friends and kept in close touch. David joined his present practice and then my husband decided he preferred a rather sexy young actress to me. So we were divorced, and I came from Swiss Cottage down to Pilgrim's Cottage. I didn't do it to get nearer David and Daphne. I think both cottages are about equidistant from them. They started to visit me here instead of there, that's all. Then Daphne became neurotic. Badly neurotic, and unable to live anything like a normal life. I'm sure that if that hadn't happened, David and I wouldn't have ... well, what I mean is, we didn't become lovers until after Daphne became ill. I suppose we both felt deprived and decided to repair the gaps in our lives."

"What did you read at university, Mrs Mace."

"Oh, the usual. English literature."

"That probably accounts for the admirable way in which you mentally précis and report these events. Now another question. Dr Bymeres made no attempt to hide his affair with you?"

"No."

"Not even from his wife?"

"We were so far away from her that distance alone ensured secrecy, I think."

"You're saying that Mrs Bymeres did not know of your liaison with her husband?"

"I'm certain of it, otherwise she wouldn't have come here, would she? And besides, David told me that Daphne had mentioned that she thought there was another woman, but she suspected it was Miss Hector, the group practice secretary."

"She definitely suspected another woman?"

"I think the whole thing was a guess on her part. She and David were no longer living as man and wife. So I suppose she imagined that David was looking elsewhere. She couldn't have been sure if she was no longer having intercourse with him, could she? On the principle that you don't miss what you don't have, I mean?"

"I would imagine not. But this Miss Hector?"

"She's a very able administrator, somewhat matronly, older than David and, judging by what he says, rather disapproving of him. Not David's type at all and not the type to be having an illicit relationship with anybody, let alone a married man and one of her employers."

Masters grinned. "I can imagine her. A good woman in every proper sense of the word. But in connection with that, one small subsidiary question. Why does Miss Hector disapprove of Dr Bymeres?"

Wanda laughed. "I really don't know. Nor does David, apparently. But I can guess why. David is a very clever doctor. Really clever. Have you ever heard of the gold-medal student? You have? Well, David's one. He's also the second opinion man in the area. Quite senior doctors consult him."

"You mean," asked Green, "for signing cremation forms and such like?"

"Oh, no. For reasons of positive medicine. To confirm a certain treatment or to modify it. A sort of extra-mural consultant, particularly among the other six or seven doctors in his own group, who really and truly don't hold a candle to him in expertise and knowledge."

"Why should Miss Hector disapprove of such a doctor."

"Because he knows he's good, I imagine. And tends not to let anybody forget it. He's ... well, he's a vain man. As well as being a perfectionist. You know, if you get a vain person who's a fool, it's laughable. But vanity coupled to outstanding ability is a totally different matter. It can be unlovable, and that, I think, is why Miss Hector is not his most fervent admirer."

Masters smiled. He knew himself to be a vain man and an able one. Yet he wouldn't have said he was unlovable. Probably that thought alone showed how mistaken he could be. Green certainly didn't love him.

The pause allowed Green to come in with a question.

"Why two single rooms for a married couple? Isn't there a double bed here? I mean, if you and Dr Bymeres sleep together, it's a bit uncomfortable on a single bed, isn't it?"

This time Wanda did blush. There had been something in Green's tone which jarred. Masters guessed she thought Green was mentally lowering her relationship with her lover to the level of a dirty story.

"I have a double bed in my room."

"Why not let them have it?"

"Because Doctor Bymeres was only going to be here for the weekend—two nights, perhaps three. It seemed pointless to go to the trouble of moving out of my room...."

"You weren't by any chance expecting the doctor to visit you of a night time, after his missus was tucked up and asleep in her single bed?"

"Hardly! That's not to say he might not have joined me had he stayed here, but I was not expecting him. Nor had we discussed whether he should not. I took it for granted that in the presence of his wife we would be circumspect, Mr Green."

"I can think of a reason why you shouldn't be."

"Really?"

"Wouldn't it have virtually forced Mrs Bymeres into divorcing her husband if she'd caught you at it? Bearing in mind that he has no evidence of infidelity to use against her to bring it about?"

"You mean...? You mean you think David had asked Daphne to divorce him so that he could marry me, but she had refused? And that finding us together herself, in the house where she herself was staying, would leave her no alternative to divorce?"

"That's it," replied Green laconically. "What's wrong with the idea?"

"It's preposterous. You're suggesting I invited Daphne down here to force her hand."

Green nodded. "All right. I'll admit to that," said Wanda surprisingly, "as long as you'll admit that if such were the case, nobody would have planned for Daphne's death, nor carried out any act to cause her to die, because such action would have been unnecessary."

"The doctor was called away."

"But he would have been back," said Wanda sweetly. "Divorce evidence secured on a Saturday night is surely as good and valid as that secured on a Friday."

Hill laughed aloud, much to Green's annoyance. Masters, too, had some difficulty in not laughing at the way this girl had turned Green's questioning about face. Green himself was cross. It showed in his face. But as Wanda continued to gaze at him, eyebrows raised interrogatively, inviting him to refute her logic, he, too, relaxed and started to grin. Then he said: "You had me there, lass."

"Thank you. Now, though it destroys completely what I have just said, I want to make it clear that never once have we discussed David getting a divorce from Daphne or marrying me."

"Never?" asked Hill.

"Never. I think we both knew the subject was taboo. I suppose we felt that if it were to happen we'd accept it. I know I did. But we'd do nothing to force it. Oh, I know it sounds ludicrous to remind you of it, but Daphne *was* my friend and the only reason why David came to me was because the woman he had loved dearly could no longer be a wife to him. What I'm trying to say is that I didn't replace Daphne in his affections, only—if Mr Green will forgive the thought—in his bed, just as he fulfilled a need of mine. If that sounds cold-blooded, please believe that it wasn't. David and I are friends who have both lost out and have ... well, I suppose I can say, comforted each other."

"By the Lord Harry," said Green, "you're a frank one."

"Why not? I have done nothing I'm very ashamed of. I didn't even rob Daphne of her husband's attentions. She no longer needed them. That, too, may sound a bit facile, but it is nevertheless true." She looked round at each one of them as she finished. Masters felt disinclined to start punching holes in this last argument of hers. There was no reason why he should at this stage. Later, perhaps, he might have to. But that would mean putting this woman through a verbal mangle, a totally unwarranted exercise while she was being as frank and helpful as now.

"Can we talk about Dr Bymeres for a moment, please, Mrs Mace? You say he had been wandering round your delightful garden after tea, and came in only after you yourself had bathed and changed for dinner."

"That's right."

"He had neither bathed nor changed by then? Seven o'clock or thereabouts?"

"No."

"Wouldn't he have to hurry if your guests were due at half past? You say he joined you in a drink. Wouldn't time be running out on him?"

"You are very sharp, Mr Masters. As a matter of fact, he hadn't changed. He was still in a dark suit, just as he'd come from surgery. I know most doctors don't worry about office suits and many wear sports jackets and flannels at work. But

62

I told you David was vain. He wore well-valeted suits and the sort of shirt that makes the tie stand out and needs links in the cuffs."

"And that is how he was dressed to go round a garden on a hot day?"

"It sounds incredible, but it's true. When he poured me a drink, he spilt a drop or two on the skirt of his jacket. He was rather put out. Although when it dried the spot wouldn't have been noticed, he said he would have to send it to be cleaned."

"That sounds to me, Mrs Mace, to be completely out of character."

"To send his suit to be cleaned?"

"No. I meant Dr Bymeres' actions. A vain man—very vain about his clothes, apparently—would have brought several sets of gear for a weekend—a hot weekend—in the country. A man as clothes-conscious as Dr Bymeres appears to be, would not have spent upwards of an hour in a garden in city clothes. He would have put on slacks and shirt. Similarly, such a man would not run himself short of time in his preparations for a dinner at which there were to be outside guests."

She frowned slightly. "I don't quite get your point."

"Don't you? I am saying that Dr Bymeres must have had a pressing reason for not changing on Friday evening. For not changing twice, in fact."

"Oh!"

"Do you know what that reason could have been, Mrs Mace?"

"Shouldn't you ask David himself?"

"Of course. But you must admit it seems as though Dr Bymeres was expecting that call before dinner. That he knew he had no reason to change."

"Oh, no! I assure you that call was genuine. It came from Miss Hector at the surgery. I took it myself. David couldn't have known it was coming."

"You said *that* call. From one so explicit as yourself Mrs Mace, I'd have expected to hear *the* call, unless, of course, there were others, or you were expecting others. Were you?"

She helped herself to another cigarette. Masters wondered if it were to give her time to consider a reply, so he did not interrupt the pause; did not press for a reply. But the business went on slightly too long.

"Come along, Mrs Mace. You have been so gratifyingly ready with your answers so far, that a long hesitation at this point leads me to believe you are hopeful of ducking the question."

"What question?" He wondered whether there actually was wariness in her eyes or whether he was imagining it because he expected it.

"Were you expecting another call concerning Dr Bymeres on Friday night?"

"After dinner. About nine thirty."

"You were expecting it?"

"I've just said so."

"What was it to be about?"

She replied immediately. "It was to have been a bogus recall."

Hill sat up, and Green sucked his teeth loudly.

"Bogus?"

"Yes."

"Why?"

"Don't you see? This was to be a break for Daphne. But David needed the break more than she did. A break from Daphne. To live with a chronic neurotic is very wearing, you know. But Daphne depended on him so much, we were sure she would not have agreed to come unless David had led her to believe he intended to stay for the weekend. But to give him as long a break as possible, we thought if he were to stay to dinner and generally settle her in and then be recalled, she would accept the situation." She turned to Green. "So you see, we really didn't intend to do any night visiting, and besides, I was very pleased to know he wouldn't be here. I'm sure we wouldn't have got through the weekend without letting slip something that would have aroused Daphne's suspicions."

"Excellent," said Green. "That helps to prove your point that you weren't hoping she'd divorce him to marry you, otherwise you'd have liked her to get suspicious."

"I suppose so."

"Who suggested the bogus call?" asked Masters.

"I think I did."

"And who suggested the weekend?"

"I definitely did that."

"Unaided? I mean did you rise to a hint from Dr Bymeres?"

"Not a direct one. He said several times that he'd like to offload Daphne somewhere for a few days, but he never suggested it should be here."

"He didn't by any chance try to veto the idea that his wife should come here when you did finally suggest it?"

"As a matter of fact, he did. But I insisted. That is why I can say that her visit here was definitely my idea."

"And when did you actually give Mrs Bymeres the invitation? You wrote inviting her, I take it?"

"No. I called on her myself last Monday afternoon. I thought she would need a bit of friendly persuasion before she would accept, and it seemed that I could do that better face to face, over a cup of tea, than in a letter or over the phone."

"Did she take much persuading?" asked Hill.

"Some. It was pretty obvious that she wanted to come, but she kept trying to invent objections. I don't know whether you've ever had dealings with a chronic depressive, but I can assure you they are hard to jolly along. They literally take themselves out of circulation at times."

"They act like mardy kids," said Green. "A woman down the street from where I live was taken that way. Wet blanket wasn't in it. Her old man was nearly driven barmy, too. He was a painter and decorator—worked for a firm. She took to ringing up the office and telling them he had to come home. So then they had to ring whichever house he was working at and tell him. Then he had to cycle back to her. Miles it was, sometimes. I know what you'd have to cope with, Mrs Mace."

"You're very understanding, Mr Green."

Whatever Masters' next question was to have been, it was not asked. The sound of tyres on the gravel path across the garden came clearly through the open window. Hill got up and looked out.

"Can't say who it is, chief, but there are two of them."

"We were only expecting Theddlethorpe, the police surgeon."

Wanda joined Hill at the window as the two men were getting out of the car. "One of them is Daphne's doctor. The one who came yesterday morning."

"Spiller?"

"That's right. David called him Rudolph—or Rudy, rather, though I must say, Dr Spiller didn't appear to like the abbreviation of his name."

The front door bell clanged. Masters was pleased to hear it was an old-fashioned bell pull, and not a modern chime. The three men left Wanda to answer. It was her house, therefore the callers, to begin with, were her visitors. She went through the glass door which led from the sitting room into the newly attached lobby and opened the main door proper. A moment later she ushered in the two men.

Masters was not surprised that Dr Spiller had not appreciated being addressed as Rudy. He was about fifty-five by Masters' guess. He was spare, rather than thin. Not over-tall, but gave no impression of being a short man. He was dressed in impeccable, tailor-made grey flannels with turn-ups and a houndstooth patterned jacket. His brown shoes were welted and boned to a high gloss. He wore a club tie with exactly the right amount of body and stiffness in it to give a knot of the correct size that would never loosen of its own volition. His face was ugly, but very symmetrical, the jowl lines scarring deep from the corners of his nose, down past a straight mouth, to the turn of the jaw bone. The nose was big. His hair—very little of it—was a swatch of grey round his ears and the back of his head. His glasses were rimless, and Masters fancied they should have been pince-nez to remain in keeping with the rest of the man's appearance. The voice—as Masters learned when Wanda introduced the newcomers—was cultured, cultivated and autocratic. At a guess he was a no-nonsense man. No patient would ever tell this man what complaint he'd got and what medicine he thought he wanted for it. Spiller would listen to an account of signs and symptoms, make his own diagnosis and then say what was what. The people on his list would knuckle under and be slightly in awe of this man, but at the same time they would have great confidence in him.

Theddlethorpe was a different type. The police surgeon was a local GP and it was Sunday afternoon. Rural GPs of his sort, on hot Sunday afternoons, wear washed-out blue jeans, deck shoes without socks, and sweat shirts with almost obliterated stencils fore and aft, extolling the virtue of walking on the Downs. Theddlethorpe was younger than Spiller—about forty, thought Masters—and he had a good deal of tightly curled gingerish hair that, though not long, grew down his neck, where it shone glossily. He was freckled, had a slight lisp, and, oddly enough, a sallow skin. His hands and forearms, too, were hairy and freckled, and Masters got the impression that he was a dedicated man who managed, nevertheless, not to take himself too seriously. At any rate, in contrast to Spiller, he grinned when introduced and when Green greeted him with the words, "Watcher, Doc," he replied with, "Watcher, Dick," which tribute to his detective activities Green accepted with good humour.

"You want to know what we've found out, Superintendent?" asked Theddlethorpe.

"Please. Perhaps we could go elsewhere to talk."

Wanda realised the implication and came in on cue. "No, don't move. I've got to go into the kitchen to clear up. The number of cups of tea your policemen have drunk today has left me with a sink full of dishes."

"Thank you."

"We won't be long, Mrs Mace," said Theddlethorpe. "Dr Spiller is in a hurry."

After Wanda had left them, Theddlethorpe added, making a general statement: "Gentlemen, Dr Spiller asked to be present at this informal meeting for reasons which will I think become obvious as we go on."

"One moment," said Masters. "I'd like to get the situation clear before we start. Are you here, Dr Spiller, because you think your professional expertise may be questioned?"

"In essence, Superintendent, yes. However, I have no doubts about the correctness of my treatment of Mrs Bymeres. My doubt is whether or not laymen will be able to interpret my professional actions correctly."

"I assure you, Dr Spiller, we should not lightly presume to doubt your expertise."

"I am sure that is so." Spiller gazed unwinkingly through his rimless spectacles. "But I feel you will understand the steps I took better if I were to explain them. That will cut out all chance of misunderstanding on your part."

"I am grateful. The better we understand all the factors in the case, the easier it will be to arrive at an accurate conclusion. Shall we sit down, gentlemen?"

As they chose seats, Masters said: "With your permission, Sergeant Hill will take notes. I find it much easier, when there are medical complications in a case, to have something with which to refresh my memory later."

Spiller, whose voice was probably more supercilious and, consequently, off-putting than he really intended it to be, hitched up one well-creased trouser leg and crossed one knee over another before commenting: "Are notes necessary in an informal conversation? This is purely a voluntary meeting on my part. I do not regard it as a session of police questioning, where a record is no doubt desirable."

The doctor's socks were held up taut on his legs, clinging to the thin shape of the ankle and the lower six or eight inches of shin. Masters found himself speculating as to whether Spiller still wore the old-fashioned suspenders, or whether those particular socks were strongly elasticated round the tops. Not that it mattered, but it hinted at a precision of mind in this man that could be useful in assessing whatever he had to say. That, in turn, sparked off an errant thought of how absurd it would seem to anybody who was told this, that a senior and successful detective should take into account the way a man wore his socks when judging the value of his contribution to an investigation.

"I agree that this discussion is to be informal and that your presence here is entirely voluntary, Dr Spiller. But if what is to be said here is going to be of no value to my colleagues and myself, we might as well forego the pleasure of the chat. If, however, it is intended to be of value—to either you or us—then I would prefer a shorthand record. We do not constitute a court of law here, so nothing that is taken down will be regarded in any way as evidence. However, it could well be the stubble of the straw from which some of the bricks of the case will eventually be made. And like stubble these days, it will be burned after being gleaned, if you so wish."

Spiller removed his glasses, to polish them on a clean, unfolded handkerchief from his trouser pocket. His eye sockets had the pale, bloodless, almost blue hue of skin that has been unexposed for years. An effect which Green had once described—in relation to prison pallor—as looking like the soles of his feet after he'd soaked them for too long in a bowl of Radox bath salts. The effect made Spiller appear defenceless, less imposing, something much less of an autocrat than formerly. So his next words were to some extent robbed of their power.

"Semantic ability in a policeman—even one of comparatively senior rank—is to be deplored. I feel that justice is best served when words are not used as a weapon, merely as a means of communication and clarification. Let your yea be yea and your nay, nay, Superintendent. Don't have us exchanging figures of speech full of simile, metaphor, comparison, allegory and parable ostensibly to enlighten a case in which I have a direct concern and in which you, as an investigating officer, and therefore also an interested party, cannot give a disinterested judgement. The emphasis of our conversation here would be wrong if you were to use your undoubted powers of verbal dissimulation and this were to be recorded. Do I make myself clear?"

"Perfectly," said Masters. "You are nervous."

"I take exception to that remark."

"Nervous that something you have done or have not done will be misconstrued as a factor contributing to Mrs Bymeres' death. Whether the professional slip—if such it is—is one of omission or commission, I don't yet know. But you are here so that when this becomes apparent, you can immediately step in to defend yourself. You say you are here voluntarily to help us. So you are. But your own professional conscience forced you to come. You dared not stay away. And I will add the hope that such direct speaking on my part will give no offence, Dr Spiller, as it was you who asked that my yea should be yea, and my nay, nay."

There was a long silence. Hill looked down at his notebook, uncomfortable in the tense atmosphere. Green was grimacing contemplatively. Theddlethorpe was watching Spiller, who in turn was glaring, speechless, at Masters. Masters sat, straight-faced, waiting for a reaction, ready for whatever form it might take. Perhaps he was the least surprised of anybody when Spiller laughed: a little titter of a laugh that bared his front teeth slightly and came forth into the quiet room like an intermittent dribble of water from an incompletely turned-off tap. Masters felt he could almost see the shape of the laugh in his mind's eye—a straight flow of sound for a few inches (or seconds) which turned inexplicably into a string of burbling sounds as small and round as petits pois, which then re-coalesced to flow away into nothing.

Theddlethorpe asked: "What's so funny, Spiller?"

Spiller turned to him, his face still bearing the signs of recent mirth. "Nothing, really, except perhaps that I have a feeling of immense relief. You see, Theddlethorpe, I am the biter bit. Daily, I set out to control my patients. To control them and yet to understand them. They feel compelled to come to me, much as Mr Masters so rightly guessed I have felt compelled to come to him. And now I find him determined to control those of us who are here. To control us and to understand us. Or at least to understand me. And that, my dear Theddlethorpe, has been a tremendous relief. To know that the Superintendent is a man who will conduct an investigation with as much concern for the people he investigates as he has for the final outcome."

Green could keep quiet no longer.

"You mean you had a poor opinion of the police, Doc?"

"I confess it. Those of us who are not in close touch with you these days must inevitably compare your falling success rate with our own increasing success rate against the evils that beset mankind."

"Interesting you should say that," replied Green. "Because there's a big difference between us, and it's this. Usually when you come up against the biggest of all evils—pain—you have the co-operation of whoever you're dealing with in order to gain success. When coppers like us come up against a big evil—like murder—we don't often get co-operation from anybody to help us be successful. So how about being different from all the rest an' being co-operative for a bit?"

Masters felt he couldn't have expressed this better himself. He felt quite pleased that circumstances had forced him to bring Green along on this case.

Chapter 5

"NOW," SAID MASTERS, "shall we finish with the preliminary skirmishing and get down to business? Mrs Daphne Bymeres died in her bed between, shall we say, nine-thirty or ten on Friday night and eight o'clock on Saturday morning. That's a wide time bracket, I know, but no doubt you two medical men will be able to narrow it appreciably when we hear what you have to tell us. All I would add at this moment is that at some unspecified time, but before midnight and possibly within an hour of Mrs Bymeres' going to bed, Mrs Mace heard a sound which she first thought was the noise of somebody retching. She dismissed this as the sound wasn't repeated, but we must now accept that her first thought could well have been right."

"Definitely," said Theddlethorpe. "The woman vomited and—we think—would have done so fairly soon after retiring. Maybe when she was sick the first time she made little noise, the contents of the stomach coming up relatively noiselessly. But later—when she was still feeling desperately sick but would have nothing to bring up—she could have made the noise of unproductive retching." He looked round the room. "We've all had that experience, surely?"

"That's right," said Green, choosing a bent Kensitas. "Where I come from, the locals describe it as flinging the pluck up. You never heard it? 'I was real bad last night. That ill, I thought I'd 'a flung me pluck up'? Very picture-skew language where I come from."

Spiller said stiffly: "I hope we can retain a little aestheticism in this conversation." Masters, used by now to Green's mannerisms and not objecting all that much to asides such as had just been heard, was unwilling to let Spiller get the autocratic

72

upper-hand. Were this to happen, it would mean that at best the conversation could become humourless and sterile, and at worst its direction could be taken out of his, Masters', hands. So the Superintendent said: "I agree with you, doctor, and so, obviously, does the DI. But whereas you see the aesthete as one who professes a superior appreciation of what is beautiful, the DI clings to the alternative but equally valid interpretation. He sees aesthetics as the science of the conditions of sensuous perception. As he has just shown, his description of retching, if a little inelegant, is—to use his own word—picture-skew, verbally at least."

Spiller accepted this silently, but with obvious bad grace. His pleasure and relief of a few moments ago had apparently gone. Masters was glad to see it. A man worried about his professional standing was to some extent softened up for questioning. A carapace of self-satisfied autocracy might be hard to crack should the need arise, whereas the witness with a niggle at the back of his mind might not be able to concentrate all his mental power for the purposes of parrying awkward questions.

"So Mrs Daphne Bymeres died. She had eaten well, and had taken a couple of glasses of wine with her dinner. But she was, I believe, in the habit of eating well and of taking the occasional drink. So there was nothing here out of the ordinary. She was also, I believe, in as good a physical shape as anybody of her years could expect to be. By that, I mean, she was a fit woman who suffered as all of us do, from time to time, from minor complaints which scarcely deserve to be classified as clinical illness. Am I right so far, Dr Spiller?"

"Quite right."

"Thank you. But Mrs Bymeres was a chronic neurotic. She suffered from severe depression. This mind sickness, I believe, did not affect her physically if we disregard any psychosomatic aspects of the case there may have been. Is that true also, Dr Spiller?"

"True, in so far as it goes."

"Where have I gone wrong?"

"In suggesting that it is possible to disregard the psycho-

73

somatic aspects. I believe that we cannot disregard them."

"Hang on a moment," said Green. "This psychosomatic business. Can a poor layman like me have that explained—in words I'd understand?"

This was Spiller's chance.

"Psychosomatic is a compound word. The psycho part relates to the mind, the somatic part to the body. So a psychosomatic affection—or illness if you prefer—has an emotional background with both mental and bodily afflictions. Many doctors—among them myself—believe strongly that there is considerable interdependence of mental processes and physical or somatic functions. That is why I believe the Superintendent would be wrong to disregard what many clinical authorities emphasise as an unvarying feature of such cases."

"You're one of these characters who says it's all in the mind? The sort who reckons that if only people believe they'll get better, they will?"

"All I say is that the mental attitude helps. But we are straying from the point. I feel that we should accept that if Mrs Bymeres had not been neurotic she might either have withstood the physical onslaught of Friday evening or, alternatively, she might have been physically and mentally capable of summoning help, which might have averted the tragedy. If the will goes in cases such as this, the body loses its normal physical response to danger."

Theddlethorpe said: "I agree with this. Everybody knows the old saw about the spirit being willing but the flesh weak. Well, the reverse of it is not true. If the spirit is weak, it doesn't make the flesh strong. It makes it weaker still. Physical response is of a low order. You'll have heard how much easier it is for a drunk to die of exposure than a sober man. There are complicated physical reasons for this, but a big contributing factor is that the brain is befuddled to a degree equating to that of a severe neurosis, and so the physical resistance to danger is impaired."

"Really," said Spiller, "I must disagree...."

"Don't bother, please, doctor," said Masters. "The analogy was merely being used to illustrate and back up your own argument. We needn't go into the effects alcohol has on blood vessels, making them more susceptible to cold."

"Very well." Masters felt that if Spiller had not been feeling a little exposed, he would never have agreed so readily. Spiller continued: "Do I take it that we are agreed that we cannot disregard the psychosomatic aspects of this case?"

Masters nodded. "As you two doctors are in agreement, we must bow to your superior knowledge, though I can't for the life of me see, as yet, what bearing it can have on the case." Privately Masters felt that Spiller's insistence on this point was entirely an effort to lessen his own culpability, should the question ever be raised. "So, we have satisfied ourselves as to the mental and physical state of Mrs Bymeres when she went to bed on Friday night, complaining of a headache." He turned again to Spiller. "Am I right in believing that Mrs Bymeres often complained of headaches?"

"Not to my knowledge."

"What does that mean exactly?" asked Hill. "Are you saying she didn't have headaches, or that she might have had them but never mentioned them to you."

"I mean the latter, of course. There is nobody who doesn't suffer from a headache from time to time. There is no family that doesn't have a home remedy for such occasions, and so the doctor never hears of them except in exceptional cases. But Mrs Bymeres was an exceptional case. She visited me regularly. At least once a month. I questioned her closely whenever she came as to how she had felt during the preceding weeks. Had she suffered from frequent and troublesome headaches I would expect to have been told about them. So, although I still adhere to my answer that if Mrs Bymeres had headaches I knew nothing of them, I am also inclined to the view that she suffered headaches very rarely, otherwise I would have heard of them."

"But," conjectured Hill, "couldn't Mrs Bymeres have been an exceptional case in another way? I mean, she was a doctor's wife. Wouldn't her husband have prescribed for her headaches?"

"I doubt it very much. It would have been most unethical

for a doctor to treat his own wife, particularly one who was under constant treatment elsewhere."

"Does that even apply to prescribing for headaches? Every man will give his own wife an aspirin or some such thing if she's got a headache. You yourself talked about home remedies."

"I see your point, Sergeant. But that in no way alters my contention that had the headaches been frequent and severe they would have been mentioned when I questioned my patient." Spiller turned to Masters. "So if it is important to your investigation to establish whether Mrs Bymeres was or was not prone to headaches, I hope you will consider what I have just said."

Masters was sure this point was important, and he felt pleased that Spiller had elucidated it in such a logical way. It made believing easy. But he felt disinclined at this moment to give the doctor the satisfaction of knowing that he had given help. A pat on the back would begin to rebuild the man's confidence and this was undesirable.

"You now see the value of notes. Sergeant Hill has got it all down, verbatim. He will make sure I bear in mind exactly what you have said."

Spiller grunted in face of this table-turning and Masters felt that one more twist of the screw had been put on the precise doctor.

"May we leave the actual business of headaches for the moment? Except in so far as to accept that Mrs Bymeres went to bed complaining of a headache which we believe to have been an unusual state of affairs in her case."

"Thank you," murmured Spiller.

"So what happened next? Can anybody see any objection to the speculation that Mrs Bymeres—apart from undressing and cleaning her teeth and generally getting ready for bed— took two doses of medicine in one form or another?"

"It would have to be two lots, wouldn't it, chief?" said Hill. "One lot prescribed by Dr Spiller that she always took, and another lot for her headache."

"We can answer that one precisely," said Theddlethorpe.

"She took her prescribed medicine and a relatively innocuous dose of two paracetamol tablets for her headache. The path lab has found the decaying traces of both drugs, and we found both bottles in her room."

"Do I take it, Doc, that we can rule out all chance of overdoses?" asked Green.

" 'Fraid so, DI," said Theddlethorpe. "And that's a pity because it would have meant that the death was suicide and this conversation and whatever comes as a result of it need never have taken place."

"What about the toxicity of the drugs you prescribed?" Green asked Spiller. "Were they killers?"

"In ordinary dosage? Certainly not."

"And you're satisfied she didn't go over the top with them?"

"Absolutely. The pathology laboratory tests show that the body contains only the prescribed dose and this is further borne out by the fact that the amount of the drug remaining in the bottle by the bedside is exactly what it should have been had the normal dose been taken."

"We seem to be clearing a lot of ground," said Masters with some satisfaction. "And what we have heard so far leads me straight back to you, Dr Spiller."

"I know what you are about to ask. Why did I refuse to sign the death certificate?"

Masters nodded.

"Even when one bears in mind the inevitable psychosomatic troubles of Mrs Bymeres, one cannot help but confess that she was nevertheless a physically healthy young woman. I had satisfied myself on this score less than a week earlier, and healthy young women in their early thirties do not die suddenly."

"No?" asked Green.

"I had not quite finished what I was saying. I was about to add that if such young women do die suddenly, then that fact alone is cause for suspicion. It is so rare an occurrence that one is in duty bound to probe very deeply for the cause."

"Point taken," said Green.

77

"So under no circumstances would I lightly have signed a death certificate. But knowing, as I did, that Mrs Bymeres had evinced none of the signs of succumbing to either of the causes which together killed her, I had to be even more circumspect. You see, had I signed, I would have been showing myself up as an inexpert bungler who, in spite of a recent and careful physical check of the patient, had not foreseen either the probability or the possibility of severe cerebral haemorrhage or heart failure."

"You can always tell these things, can you?" Green selected another Kensitas. "What I'm aiming at, Doc, is clarifying my own mind, because I always thought that the onset of cerebral bleeding was always rapid and sudden, like. Any time, any place, any body. We're all liable and nobody knows when."

"That is correct as far as it goes."

"Then how will a check-up a week earlier help you to foresee it?"

Spiller again grinned his little smile. He was on his subject now, and he was recovering some of his poise. "Because there are certain predisposing factors, Mr Green. Apart from age, because it is in the more elderly that one would expect cerebral haemorrhage, the signs one must watch for are hypertension and atheroma. Now, when I say hypertension, I mean severe hypertension. Mrs Bymeres did, in fact, have slight hypertension, but then so have many otherwise healthy people. And atheroma ... do you know what that is?"

"Tell me!"

"It's a degenerative change of the arteries—what you would call hardening of the arteries—and is a disease of late middle life and old age. A fatty degeneration of the arteries if you like to regard it as such, where lipids—which are a group of fat-like substances in the blood—have infiltrated the walls of the arteries and robbed them of elasticity—or hardened them. The blood gets sluggish and can't get through the blocked blood vessels, so you will appreciate that just as a swollen or blocked river overflows its banks, so blood will haemorrhage from blocked arteries."

"I get it."

"You do? Then you will appreciate that a doctor can at least assess the likelihood of cerebral haemorrhage."

"Mrs Bymeres had no atheroma?" asked Masters.

"The blood test showed her to be comfortably inside the acceptable bracket, and as I say, her blood pressure was only marginally up."

"What about her heart?" asked Green. "Can you be sure of that, too? Heart attacks are pretty sudden, too."

"Again there are predisposing factors or signs which would lead one to anticipate imminent cardiac failure. No doctor could miss them, and no doctor would allow them to go untreated—at least by rest if not by drugs. Believe me, Mrs Bymeres had no bradycardia, tachycardia, fibrillation, flutter, ventricular asystole or any sign which would lead one to expect the slightest degree of heart disease, let alone massive cardiac failure. In these circumstances, one must ask oneself why the heart should fail."

"A question which you felt must be answered by a more thorough investigation than you would normally make before issuing a death certificate?"

"Quite. Oh, I could have told you why the heart failed. But I couldn't have told you what caused the causes."

"Ah!" Masters was interested. Spiller had said 'what caused the causes'. He, as investigating officer, would have to go one step even further back. What caused the causes that caused ... it was like trying to imagine the universe. If God caused the big bang that caused the heavenly bodies to fly outwards, what caused God in the first place?

"Ah! Why did the heart fail?"

"The clinical picture of acute failure is very similar to that which occurs in peripheral circulatory failure or shock, and that means there is a decrease in the circulating blood volume. This may be due to a number of causes, among which would be the haemorrhage and indeed, the vomiting, which results in a loss of fluid and electrolytes—notably the chloride ion. The excessive sweating has similar effects. As a result there is a lack of venous return to the heart and, therefore of the cardiac output. Everything then closes down,

79

as it were. That is an over-simplified explanation, of course, but I have merely described the signs which caused me to suspect acute cardiac failure even in a dead woman without benefit of post-mortem or laboratory tests. I could not, however, sign a death certificate without more thorough investigation as to why these things should have happened. So I called the police, knowing that their own medical man would be called in to resolve the problem."

"The clinical problem, perhaps."

"That is, of course, what I meant. I had no intention of suggesting that your role in this affair would be superseded."

"Thank you. Now we know exactly why Dr Spiller saw fit to involve the police, the questions open to us grow fewer. In fact there remains only one. And that relates to the medication Mrs Bymeres was receiving at the hands of Dr Spiller. Would you care to tell us, Dr Spiller, what drugs you were prescribing for her?"

Masters knew immediately that he had reached or was heading straight for the chink in Spiller's armour. The doctor wiped his forehead with the neatly folded handkerchief and, thereafter, seemed not to know what to do with his hands. This was the stage which Masters had aimed to reach with Spiller. But suddenly, a feeling of pity for the man overcame him. Spiller was a professional. A conscientious professional otherwise he would not be present. And he had showed he knew his stuff. And yet here he was, dreading the next few minutes. It was this that caused Masters to change his tactics. He decided to cheer the doctor up—to restore some of the lost confidence.

"But before you tell us what treatment you were giving Mrs Bymeres, I would like you to know that every one of us here appreciates the fact that doctors, as a rule, are very particular as to which person they choose as a GP for themselves and their families. Dr and Mrs Bymeres chose you, so it is fair to assume they had a high opinion of you, and as I have been given to understand that Dr Bymeres is, himself, a medical man of acknowledged outstanding ability, it is also fair to assume that their choice was not solely on account of your pleasant bedside manner, but also on account of your clinical expertise. I say this, because during informal talks such as we are now having it helps if all parties are aware of the standing each enjoys in the discussion."

Spiller was obviously gratified by this speech. He thanked Masters and relaxed visibly in his chair. The restless-hands syndrome ended. The man became a competent and confident witness. Green seemed to sense this, too. He leaned towards Spiller. "Doc," he said earnestly, "don't make it too technical, otherwise you're going to set off some of that psychosomatic stuff you were talking about earlier."

"Oh? How is that Mr Green?"

"Well, it's like this. I have a very good memory, see? But it's the sort of memory that remembers faces, names, dates, places and ordinary everyday events. It has a nasty habit of rejecting what it doesn't understand—like medical jargon, for instance. So where does that leave me? I'll tell you. Most nights, when I go to bed, I don't count sheep, I go over in my mind all the evidence I've heard that day, and before I can get round to thinking about it, I drop off to sleep. But when it comes to technical guff, I can't remember the words, so my brain gets too active, flogging itself to death in an effort to remember. Then I can't get to sleep. So next day I'm tired—in body and mind. Sort of psychosomatic, wouldn't you say?"

Spiller gave his little grin of amusement. "It certainly could become so, Mr Green. But could I prescribe in advance for such an unfortunate eventuality?"

"Go ahead."

"A double scotch on retiring would fill the bill, I think."

"I can see now why other doctors pick you to look after them. Keep it all as simple as that, and I'll understand it well enough."

"I will do my best." Spiller turned towards Masters. "You already know that I have been treating Mrs Bymeres for the last eighteen months or two years for a severe neurosis which, to satisfy Mr Green, we will call chronic depression. But I must state at the outset that chronic depression is rather a loose term to cover a complex neurosis of long standing and embodying a large number of symptoms."

"Such as, doctor?"

"You want me to spell them out?"

"If it doesn't grow too complicated and take too long."

Spiller was now in his element. Like any other man, he obviously enjoyed holding forth on some aspect of his own subject to others less knowledgeable than himself. He frowned slightly with the concentration needed to cut his account short and keep it simple.

"In this case there was a great degree of apathy, with delusions which I diagnosed as self-condemnatory and slightly hypochondriacal. Her personality really had disintegrated, though Mrs Bymeres had not become lax in personal cleanliness despite a noticeable dropping off in appearance. I put this last down to apathy—she just couldn't be bothered to shop for new clothes or to visit her hairdresser."

Hill asked: "What caused it, doctor?"

"Who knows? Some unhappy experience, perhaps. But I think not."

Masters asked: "Could it have been continued unhappiness over a longer period? Or imagined unhappiness. So many women these days are said to be so disillusioned with their lot that they could be said to live almost in a state of continuous discontent."

"That is a more likely explanation, Superintendent." Spiller was now leaning forward earnestly. "But it is so difficult to be sure. The manifestations differ in virtually every case. As you know, Mrs Bymeres never lost her appetite, even though her apathy meant that her physical activity was curtailed."

"Could I come in there?" asked Theddlethorpe. "A thought just struck me. If she ate well—as the worried often do—but her physical activity was retarded, wouldn't she develop chronic constipation from time to time?"

"Oddly enough, she didn't. She was a great fruit and salad eater, so this probably saved her. But I can see your point, Theddlethorpe. Chronic constipation would have led to frequent occipital headaches. But I can assure you she never complained of either, and I never treated her for them."

Theddlethorpe nodded. "The pathologist bears you out. Not in so many words, but he makes no mention of undue stomach content."

"Excellent," said Masters. "It's wonderful how bits and pieces can fall into place when there's some form of cross-check such as that. So, Dr Spiller, what were you doing for Mrs Bymeres?"

"Apart from arranging psychological treatment, there wasn't a lot I could do for her, except to see her frequently and to give her the usual tranquillisers such as diazepam—Valium, you know—chlorpromazine and so on."

"Why see her frequently if there was little you could do?"

"To show her that she was being cared for and thought about. Such people must not be left to suppose that nobody gives a damn about them. That would worsen their mental state."

"I see you were most conscientious over this aspect of therapy, doctor. But one more question. You said you prescribed the usual tranquillisers. You mentioned two by name. Do I take it that you varied the drug treatment from time to time?"

Spiller leaned back and didn't answer for a moment. It seemed to Masters that he was taking some care over choosing his next words. This, then, was the sticky patch. The moment Spiller had not been looking forward to. But at any rate the man was now confident, even if he was not dominating the scene.

"Yes, I varied it. I am a great believer in what are known as 'drug holidays' in neurotic cases. Perhaps I should explain the reasoning behind my approach." He was going slowly, thoughtfully, and, sensing this, no one attempted to interrupt him. "Quite simply, it is this. I believe that if a patient is maintained on drug A—and by maintained, I mean the patient and his illness being kept in as good a state of control as possible—it does no harm, and often a lot of good to put him on drug B for a few weeks. This stops the patient becoming too dependent on drug A and, more important, it stops him getting a tolerance for the drug."

"Dependence I understand," said Masters. "Anybody who has had to deal with drug addition is only too well aware of it. But tolerance! What exactly is meant by that in this context?"

"Simply that the body learns to tolerate regular amounts of a drug. And when the body begins to tolerate it, then the drug loses its effectiveness. It's akin to cold baths. If you are not used to taking them, the body reacts strongly if you step into one. But if you take a cold bath every day of the year the body learns to tolerate them. In other words, it takes no notice."

"That's logical," said Green. "What's the answer?"

"There is a choice. One can go ahead with the same drug in increased amounts to get the same effect, or one can change the drug. But if one would prefer to continue drug A, one must pre-empt toleration by a drug holiday. One changes the drug for a short time at an opportune moment. Done correctly, this will allow one to maintain the patient for the longest possible time on the drug of choice without any undue increase in tolerance or dependence."

Hill said: "A change is as good as a rest?"

"More or less. Hence the term drug holiday."

Masters asked quietly: "Was Mrs Bymeres on a drug holiday?"

"Unfortunately, she was."

"When had you changed her medicine?"

"The Saturday before she died, when I gave her the check-up. I changed her medicine completely and put her on M.A.O.I.s."

"On what?" asked Green.

"Monoamine oxidase inhibitors."

"I know! The things you mustn't eat cheese with."

"Ah!" said Masters. "And she made a hearty meal on Friday evening. But I have a feeling that it's not all going to be quite as simple as that, is it Dr Spiller?"

"No."

"Because you warned her not to eat cheese, didn't you?"

"Most emphatically."

"And," said Theddlethorpe, "she didn't."

"I thought so," said Masters. "But we're sidetracking. You hadn't finished what you were saying, Dr Spiller."

"No, no I hadn't." Spiller again seemed much less sure of himself. So much so that he tended to rush into an explanation that struck Masters almost as an apology. Almost vindicatory.

"Apart from her depression, Mrs Bymeres was a pretty healthy specimen as you already know. But, as has been said, her mental state curtailed her physical activity, and so she was getting out of condition."

"That figures," said Green.

"And so—again as I've already mentioned—she was getting a touch of blood pressure. Nothing too great, but I felt that I should attempt to counteract it as soon as it showed, otherwise it could grow to serious proportions. So I changed her medicine to take care of the problem."

"The M.A.O.I. you mentioned."

"Exactly."

"But if M.A.O.I.s are anti-depressive, where does the treatment for blood pressure come in?"

Theddlethorpe said: "Hear him out, Superintendent."

"Of course. I'm sorry. Please go on, doctor."

"I wanted Mrs Bymeres to have a drug holiday from her tranquillisers, so I immediately considered M.A.O.I.s. But there was also the hypertension problem, and M.A.O.I.s are tricky drugs in that they don't much like being mixed with other drugs. Just as they don't like cheese. So I was naturally a bit wary of giving Mrs Bymeres a second medicine for her hypertension. But fortunately, some M.A.O.I.s do two jobs. They're effective in depression and hypertension. So I prescribed an M.A.O.I. expecting it to perform both functions."

"Very neat, that," murmured Hill.

"It is," said Theddlethorpe, "until you hit an unforeseen snag."

"Like eating cheese?"

"That's right. But as Spiller has told you, he warned Mrs Bymeres not to eat cheese, and the first question both he and I asked Mrs Mace when we arrived on Saturday morning was whether she had eaten cheese. Mrs Mace swore that there was no cheese on her table in any shape or form."

"So that was why you refused to sign the certificate, Dr Spiller?"

"One of the reasons, certainly. Had she eaten cheese, the death could have been explained easily enough."

"If she had eaten cheese—unsuspectingly, perhaps, in a cheese sauce, say—what is there about it which would cause intracranial haemorrhage and cardiac arrest?"

Spiller said: "The ingestion of tyramine, which is the constituent of cheese that causes the trouble. Tyramine is not in itself a poison, but we can say, for the sake of clarity, that it has a form of mechanical action." He looked apologetically towards Green. "If I am to explain its action, you must forgive me if I get a little technical, though I shall try to make it as understandable as possible to the layman."

Green nodded his understanding and agreement. Spiller continued. "Monoamine oxidase inhibitors are indirect stimulants for the treatment of depression. By indirect, I mean they work in a rather roundabout way. But you can understand that one needs to use a stimulant for depression, can't you? Like a man who has a whisky to buck him up if he's feeling low?"

"That's clear so far."

"Well, as I say, M.A.O.I.s are indirect stimulants and work in a roundabout way. What they do—as their name implies—is to inhibit the body's production of monoamine oxidases. As soon as this production is curtailed, the body accumulates more than the usual amounts of some other things like serotonin and one I'm sure you've heard of—noradrenaline. These are the substances which give the lift, by means of a very diverse and complex mixture of physiologic and pharmacologic activity in the body. One of these effects is to constrict the blood vessels to get things working better, much the same as you might restrict air intake to a motor car engine on a cold morning. All of which is very fine, but you know as well as I do that even so, if you give a car engine too rich a mixture, you choke it. The works get flooded and gummed up and it stops."

"Where does tyramine come in?"

"Tyramine has the sort of mechanical action I spoke of earlier. It increases the mechanical activity until it causes things to stop."

Theddlethorpe agreed. "That's it in simple terms. Tyramine doesn't poison the body, but it overworks some of the systems till you get too much blood going through—just as you can get too much petrol in your car. As a result, you get severe hypertensive reactions by the body—in other words, dangerously high blood pressure."

"As a result of which," guessed Masters, "the patient would get a massive headache."

"Quite right," said Spiller. "That's one of the characteristics. Eventually, this rapid and prolonged rise in blood pressure means something has to give. The result is intracranial haemorrhage or cardiac failure or—as in this case—both."

"Thank you," said Masters. "We realise that this must be a complicated medical problem, but I think we have got the gist of it."

"There's just one more thing. Basically—all you need to know in such cases—the trouble is that the body gets too much nitrogen. The other thing you must realise is that tyramine is an organic compound containing nitrogen, and so should be avoided at all costs."

"That seems fairly clear. We now know how she died, or rather what caused the trouble. But we have not been told how the tyramine got into the body to set all this in motion."

Spiller took off his glasses and started to polish them again. Without looking at Masters, he said: "Cheese isn't the only food that contains tyramine."

"The devil it isn't! But it was the only one you warned Mrs Bymeres against specifically?"

Spiller nodded. "It's common practice to warn against
87

cheese. It is by far the major culprit. But there is quite a list of foods containing tyramine to a lesser degree. These are not usually mentioned to patients because," he spread his hands, "because they are not usually dangerous, and it would restrict the ordinary diet abominably. That, however, is no excuse for me. I should have given her the list...."

"Please don't distress yourself, Dr Spiller. What has happened is over. You may feel you are to blame because your patient ate one of these proscribed foods, but...."

"One!" exclaimed Theddlethorpe. "My dear Super, the whole bloody menu was comprised of tyramine-bearing foods. Even the wine."

"What's that?"

"Every single dish contained tyramine foods. And that woman ate hearty. She took enough of the stuff to kill ten people like herself."

Masters pinched his nose. He looked across at Spiller. "I think, doctor, we can safely say you could not have foreseen this." Then he looked at Theddlethorpe. "What was on the menu?"

"Cold consommé made with yeast extract, game pâté, liver and bacon with whole broad beans, lemon mousse—all washed down with chianti."

"That sounds a very down-to-earth sort of meal."

"Maybe it does. But yeast extract, game, beef liver, whole broad beans, citrus fruit and chianti all contain tyramine. Man, if you set out to kill a patient on M.A.O.I.s you couldn't have planned it better."

Masters grimaced.

"Isn't it because we are sure somebody did plan it that we are all here?"

Chapter 6

THE MEETING BROKE up immediately after Masters' last remark. While the others left the sitting room by the front door, he went through to the kitchen to tell Wanda they were leaving. He found her sitting on a stool at the table, on which was spread a newspaper and various bits of silver—cruet, tea service, forks and spoons. She was wearing stained old working clothes and an apron, and was busily polishing away.

"We're going now, Mrs Mace. But I shall be back again tomorrow."

She stopped what she was doing. The westering sun was now coming through the window of the kitchen that looked over the plough behind the house. The red beams were gilding her hair and highlighting the delicate structure of her long face. She wasn't beautiful, perhaps, but she was more than just a good-looking woman. Oddly enough the old gloves and the apron did not detract from the picture. He found himself staring hard at her as though she were something that had drawn his interest in an art gallery or shop window.

"I expected you would come back."

"Why?"

"This is a bit nightmarish, isn't it? And nightmares return." She suddenly blushed. "Oh, I beg your pardon, that was terribly rude of me, but I hope you know what I mean."

"I understand." He found himself loth to go. "That's an odd occupation for a bright, sunny Sunday evening."

"You were in the sitting room," she reminded him.

"So we were. I hope we didn't put you out—figuratively as well as literally."

She smiled. "Of course not."

"Are you expecting Dr Bymeres?"

"Not tonight."

He never knew what made him make the suggestion, but he said: "We are staying at the Four-Fingered Hand. Would you care to join us for dinner?"

"Not for dinner, thank you. I don't think I shall eat very much tonight."

"If not for dinner, what about after dinner? For a drink? Say nine o'clock?"

Again she smiled. "Is that an official request?"

"No. And I promise not to talk about ... nightmares, if you'll come."

"I'd love to. I will meet you in the Missing Finger bar."

"The Missing Finger?"

"They name their bars. Thumb bar, Forefinger bar and so on. But as they've got five bars, one has to be the Missing Finger."

"Right. See you at nine."

"With or without Mr Green?"

"What do you think?"

He left by the kitchen door and climbed into the car. "What happened?" asked Green. "Couldn't you find her."

"She was in the kitchen, cleaning silver. I stayed to have a word so that our departure wouldn't appear too abrupt."

Hill moved off and headed down the gravelled way.

"I wonder if she knows she fed her pal the stuff that killed her?"

"At the moment, I don't think she does. But I shall try to keep an open mind."

"And what does that mean?"

"It means I don't think she was implicated in this business and, because of that, I could be in danger of assuming that she wasn't."

"So what are you going to do about it?"

"I've invited her to have a drink at our pub tonight to try to get to know her better."

"You reckon that's the reason?"

"I hope so. This is my reasoning. She is a very intelligent woman. She is apparently frank and honest. She also struck me as being terribly naïve for an educated woman of the world who has divorced one man and openly consorts with a married doctor. Now, tell me, is that a correct assessment, or am I being fooled up to the hilt? I want to know and know quickly. Preferably before we start tomorrow's little games."

"I'd say that was fair enough, but you can't get away from the fact that she's a damn' good-looking woman."

"She is. And I want to know whether that is colouring my thinking."

Surprisingly, Green said: "I wouldn't have thought so. I've known you go overboard for a woman only once before, and that was for the girl who got three years for manslaughter." Masters frowned. The memory was painful. But Green, with about as much finesse as a Tiger tank, forged ahead. "Remember her? You went ahead and put her in the dock. That surprised a lot of us, because the whisper was that you'd intended to marry her."

"Shut it!" growled Hill from the front seat.

"Why? Have I said something I shouldn't?"

"Oh no! Only put your big foot in it."

Green turned to Masters with a look of surprise on his face. "Look, I was only trying to reassure you...."

"I know. Thank you."

"Then what...?"

"I'll tell you," said Masters. "I did ask her to marry me after she got out. She got full remission, so she was free in a couple of years. I was told that a Yard man could not marry a convicted criminal and still remain a Yard man."

"And you chickened out? I don't believe it."

"I resigned."

"You what? I'll bet they wouldn't accept that. Their blue-eyed boy!"

"I insisted they accept it. But the lady in question somehow got to know of what she called 'the price I was having to pay to marry her' and backed out. She emigrated and has since married."

"She got to know?" growled Green. "How? Did you tell her?"

"No."

91

"Then some rotten bastard ... hey! One of the nobs made sure she knew."

"That's what I believe. But she would never tell me, and I've been unable to find out who it was."

"So you withdrew your resignation."

"There seemed little point in not doing so."

"Well, if they kept your resignation a secret, it shows they were angling to get it withdrawn before anybody knew. And I'll tell you something else. Knowing you, they'd never have approached your intended themselves."

"I don't follow."

"They knew that if they did, you'd be on to them like a sparrow on to a crumb. So they'd do it through a third party. The one who approached your girlfriend wouldn't be one of the four or five senior coppers you'd be able to identify immediately if she made a chance remark. It'd be somebody else who you didn't know, carefully briefed."

Masters sat quite still for a moment, unlit pipe in one hand, matches in the other. Then he said quietly: "Thanks, Greeny," and proceeded to light the pipe.

Hill glanced round at Green and they exchanged eye signals. A moment or two later the car turned on to the main road and immediately thereafter Hill swung it into the covered coachway which bisected the ground floor of the inn. Over the years a lot of glass had replaced panels in doors, and the original cobbled square in the heart of the building had been glazed over. Despite the heat of the day, the area was cool and shady. Indoor plants were growing in large tubs, cordoned up the walls and even on to wires overhead. It was these runners which, together with hanging baskets of geraniums, gave the shade and the sense of green colour. A small fountain splashed in one corner, and the sound of it, coming loud after the engine was switched off, gave a novel welcome to the traveller.

"You can't leave it here," said Green. "This is a public right of way."

"There's a double gate ahead leading to garages. When we've clocked in I'll get them to open it up."

Green descended and stretched. "Now what shall I do first?" he said aloud. "Order a pint, have a piddle, or go and see if the receptionist's got a nice pair of sooper-doops?"

"Fair division of labour," said Masters. "I'll book us all in. Hill can order us all a beer, and you can have your piddle. Have one for all three of us while you're at it."

They entered the Four-Fingered Hand by a side door leading from the covered way. Green saw the sign he was looking for straight away and left the other two to continue on their way.

Masters guessed the receptionist was the daughter of the house. There was no doubt she was a pretty girl of about twenty, with a thin face and long dark hair. But she wouldn't have suited Green, who liked his females well filled-out. This one was so slender that her bones stood proud on her bare shoulders, elbows and wrists. Under the thin blouse Masters could see the outline of a bra which could only have been there for modesty's sake. It certainly wasn't needed for anything other than moral uplift.

"The rooms are all at the back," she said apologetically. "They weren't booked until very late today."

"I know. Please don't worry. We're lucky to have got in at all I suppose."

"You are, really, especially at a weekend. I'll show you up."

Green joined them. He was patently disappointed in her. "How," he whispered to Masters, "can a girl as nice looking as that be so thin? Put an arm round her waist and you'd break her in two or more. There's not enough fat on her to fry an egg."

The stairs were shallow and creaky; the passages low and dim; the rooms timbered and without a right angle in their construction. But it was 'nice'. Green said so. "Nice, this! It's what every pub in England should be like."

It was eight o'clock when they sat down to dinner. Green tucked his napkin into his collar before taking the menu. "This is where I've got to be careful," he said. "None of your tyramine stuff for me."

93

Hill scoffed. "What have you got to worry about?"

"Quite a lot," replied Green. "I was made redundant yesterday remember. That's bad enough, innit?"

"Sorry. I meant about your food?"

"I get terrible indigestion at times."

"That's not due to any kind of inhibitor," said Masters, "but to total inhibition." He ordered his meal and the others followed suit.

When the waiter had gone, Green said: "About that menu on Friday night. It could just have happened that way."

"Agreed," said Masters. "I would hate to work out the chances of every course of a four course meal—five if we add the wine—being loaded with tyramine, but I would say, offhand, that a million to one would be a good spec. And if we were to try to work out what the chances are of that million to one spec being fed to a woman on M.A.O.I., then the figure becomes so astronomical that one just can't accept it."

"How do you mean, accept?" asked Hill. "Do you mean that the mind can't grasp the figure or you don't believe the meal was prepared by chance?"

The waiter served large slices of iced melon, cut across and garnished with a slice of orange and a cherry. As he again left, Masters said: "I really meant the former, but I suppose I mean both."

Green scattered powdered ginger freely over his melon.

"So you're not going to believe it though it could just conceivably be chance—no matter what the odds?"

"Say we accept the odds," said Masters popping the cherry on its stick into his mouth, "what about the other factors?"

"What factors?"

"First, the serving of broad beans in their hulls. Oh, I know it's done and one could say that it's a habit which may be gaining a foothold, but as yet, in my experience, the likelihood of coming across whole broad beans is slim. Ordinary broad beans are not all that common. In the pods—one could go for a month of Sundays without encountering them."

"But they're not unknown."

"Admittedly. But when one realises that broad beans as normally eaten do not contain tyramine, whereas the pods do, and the pods appeared on a menu chock-full of tyramine and specially chosen and prepared for a guest to whom tyramine is an absolute killer, what then?"

"I get you," said Green. "I'll go along with it." He started to scrape the now bare melon skin with his spoon. "Don't cut these very carefully, do they? Lots of good stuff left here."

"What else, chief?" asked Hill.

"I put the chianti second. Now, I may be prejudiced here because I don't care for the stuff myself. But I would have said it was the last wine a woman would have chosen for a dinner party. I have never been out to a meal in a house where it has been served. So I'm counting it an oddity, particularly in this context, as it seems to be the only wine with a big tyramine content."

Green put down his spoon. "It's dry and rough," he announced. "I had it in Italy during the war, and I tell you that some of the squaddies wouldn't take it even though there was nothing else available. I can't see any woman choosing it as the best wine to serve to elderly people and a sick woman without some very good reason. And I guess the reason was because of the tyramine."

"Any other factors, chief?"

"I find it surprising that no cheese was offered at that dinner party."

"So do I," said Hill, "seeing that's the major culprit."

Green snapped his fingers and leaned across towards Masters. "You think it was left out on purpose because to have provided it would have been going over the top?"

"Something of the sort. Mrs Bymeres wouldn't have eaten it anyhow, because she'd been warned against it. But with men at the table ... well, a hostess will usually have a cheese board just in case anybody wants to top up at the end or prefers not to take a sweet. But if the hostess could foresee the necessity in the near future of putting a hand on her heart and saying: 'There was no cheese at my table', what then?"

The waiter placed a large grilled sole in front of Green and plates of cold turkey in front of Masters and Hill. The conversation ceased until all had been fully served.

"I think I see what you mean, chief. It sounds as if somebody wasn't expecting an examining doctor to enquire about anything but cheese. As if somebody would ask about what Mrs Bymeres had eaten and see nothing alarming in all those things she did eat."

Masters, mixing oil and vinegar, nodded.

"Some hope," grunted Green. "They must have known there'd be an enquiry and that the pathologist would suss it all out."

"Would there have been an enquiry if Spiller had signed the death certificate of a woman on whom he had been in constant attendance for the past eighteen months?"

"P'raps not. Definitely not, in fact. But somebody must have thought Spiller pretty green."

Masters put his knife and fork down.

"Spiller was a worried man today."

"Nervous as a kitten."

"Why?"

"Why? Because he knew he'd made a bloomer in only telling Mrs Bymeres to lay off the cheese." He stopped and looked up with understanding dawning in his eyes.

"Go on."

"Cripes. She tells somebody who knows about these things —her husband—that Spiller had ordered her not to eat cheese. 'Only cheese?', asks hubby. 'Only cheese', she replies. But hubby knows about broad beans in their skins an' chianti an' liver all containing tyramine an' jumps to the conclusion that Spiller doesn't. So she's fed the verboten foods with the inevitable result an' Spiller is called in. But he doesn't just ask about cheese because he does know about these other things he's forgotten to mention. Result? He gets the jitters over his own negligence, but he's still got enough guts to call in the police instead of just calmly signing a death certificate which would have let him off the hook. Bully for Spiller and headache for whoever misjudged him."

96

Hill said: "Chief, shall I be expected to think like that when I go to a Division?"

"It comes with practice, and if you get somebody like the DI to back you up by cottoning on before you've even explained yourself, you'll do all right."

"Besides, lad," said Green, comfortingly, "one or other of us will always be available at the end of a telephone to help you out when you need it."

"Thanks," said Hill drily. He turned to Masters. "I'll try my 'prentice hand now, chief. What you've just said implicates Mrs Mace and Dr Bymeres."

"If true, yes."

"Conspiracy?"

"Could be."

"She did the cooking."

"He could have chosen the menu."

"I bet he didn't," said Green.

"Why not?" asked Hill.

"Because he was originally going to be there for supper, and if he had been there he'd have had to stop his wife eating that grub."

"But he *wasn't* there for supper. He was called away."

"On a true bill call which he couldn't have known about."

"Then you reckon we've got the murderer—Mrs Mace?"

"Could be. She obviously has a yen for Bymeres. Why not remove the only obstacle? Means, method and motive, lad. She had them all, and that's all we need for a case against her."

Hill looked bewildered. "But less than an hour and a half ago, when we left Pilgrim's Cottage, you were saying—in so many words—that she wasn't guilty."

"Wrong. I didn't say anything like that. I wondered whether she knew she had fed her pal the stuff that killed her and it was the Super who said, 'At the moment I don't think she does, but I shall try to keep an open mind'."

"Well, if the chief doesn't think so...."

"He didn't then. But he said to keep an open mind an'
97

now, as a result of further discussions, the opinion of an hour and a half ago has changed."

"Has it, chief?"

"The opinion may have changed, but the mind hasn't closed. I was too impressed by her apparent honesty to come too hastily to a conclusion."

"In that case," said Hill, "isn't it dangerous to invite a suspect to a social meeting? You've always told us, chief, never to get personally involved."

"That's true. But I think I've always been a firm believer in meeting anybody on his or her own ground. That's a pretty loose sort of statement, but I'll arrange to meet a suspect builder's labourer in a public bar if I think that is the best milieu for the encounter, so why not treat a suspect woman in the same way if she is accustomed to patronising a cocktail bar?"

"Put like that it sounds all right, but I got the impression earlier that you yourself thought you might be getting involved because she's a good-looker."

"I'm a man, Sergeant. What man doesn't feel drawn to a good-looking woman of character? And it's the last bit I'm worried about. Character. In my case it is a greater lure than the good looks, although I'm willing to admit that the good looks do make character more powerful than it would be otherwise."

"At least you recognise the danger," said Green, wiping his mouth. "And that should be a good enough safeguard. But there's just one thing that bugs me."

"Oh, what's that?"

"I can't get interested in a woman who has slept around. Now take this Wanda bird. She had a husband, then she took a lover. I could never fancy being third mate on a drifter."

"I'm the same," said Hill.

Masters considered the point. Both his colleagues were obviously of the type who expected a woman to save herself until they happened along. What, he wondered, would be their attitude if they were to meet Wanda Mace in different circumstances where they didn't know she had been Bymeres' mistress? He guessed they would overlook the divorce. Why? Rectification of a mistake? Increased availability?

Masters got to his feet. "It's almost nine o'clock. If I'm any judge, Mrs Mace will include promptitude among her graces. I'll see you gentlemen later."

He had just located the Missing Finger bar when he heard, through the open entrance of the inn, the arrival of a car which he imagined could be a Mini. He paused for a few moments. Then she appeared in the doorway. It was still daylight, but the passageway to the door was lit with wall candlelights. They allowed him to see—as a silhouette would not have done—that her long dress was in some shiny material—he guessed at Thai silk—with diagonal broad stripes of blue, silver and red. They were made more striking by being registered in narrow black lines. Her very fair hair was simply done, drawn back from her forehead and falling in a cascade over the halter top of the bodice on to her bare back.

He went to meet her.

"I hope I haven't kept you waiting?"

"We are both so right on time we might have synchronised our watches as if for a military operation."

She smiled warmly. "We're not about to assume either offensive or defensive positions, I hope?"

He opened the bar door and ushered her in. "Can there possibly be a meeting of the sexes without tactical postures —in the military sense?"

She didn't answer immediately. It was as though she realised that her entrance would cause interest. The stares from men seated on stools at the counter! The appraising glances from women seated with their men-folk at the tables! She refrained from speaking, as if to carry on the conversation might rob her appearance of some of its impact. He reckoned she had an aura, which tacitly implied that she was a symbol of what the human race could produce if only it would try hard enough to improve its stock. Masters, who had much the same tip about himself, dwarfed her, though she was tall; and he knew that together they would catch any eye that still had the power to see and appreciate.

"Horse's neck, please," she replied in answer to his offer of a drink as they took a window table. "Very long and very cold."

When he returned with the drinks, she said: "Ever since you invited me here, I've been wondering why I accepted and what was your real purpose in asking me to come."

He offered her a cigarette from the packet he had armed himself with earlier. As he then packed his pipe—having sought and been given her permission to smoke it—he said: "Could we not just assume that it was one of those spur of the moment impulses on my part for asking, and yours for agreeing to come?"

"I'll agree that we were both impulsive. But I can claim that the events of the last forty-eight hours have left me in sore need of cheer. I had before me the choice of an evening alone in a depressing house or a break in pleasant company. So I can rationalise my impetuosity. Can you do the same?"

"Is it vital that I should?"

"I think so. You see, Mr Masters, this is a totally new experience for me."

"Having a drink with a policeman?"

"Coming out without knowing why. Always before, I've known exactly why men other than my husband or David have invited me to spend the evening with them. And I'm not being big-headed in assuming that, because most personable women have the same experience. Whether the men in question are fast or slow workers, such invitations are inevitably part of the groundwork for spending—or so they hope—not just an evening with them, but a night, too."

Masters smiled, but said nothing.

She looked straight at him. "So what do you want, Mr Masters? To bed me or grill me?"

"You tell me."

"Neither. I don't believe you want the former, and I am certain you promised to avoid the latter."

"So I did, but you are wrong."

"You want to question me about Daphne's death."

"No. When you said neither, it would have been nearer the mark to say both. But that doesn't mean that I shall attempt either course of action. To tell you the truth—and please don't regard that as the preamble to a lie—I am not averse to attractive women, and the sight of you alone and doing household chores on such an evening as this struck me as a waste of an attractive woman. As I am also averse to waste, I did what I could to avoid it. I invited you here."

She toyed with her glass for a moment, and then without looking up at him, she asked: "Are you a lonely man, Mr Masters?"

"What do I say to that? I suppose I must be. I'm unmarried. Not from choice—in that I would wish to be married—but more from lack of chance, in that the woman I wished to marry would not accept me."

"Was she free to do so?"

"Yes. But she thought that she would ruin my career."

"She must have loved you a lot."

"I think she did. And I think that knowledge has made me lonelier than ever."

"Loneliness is a state of mind, isn't it? I knew Daphne was lonely. Her mind had shut her off from everything. She was a mental hermit who had known what it was not to be lonely and who still cherished the memories of being loved. Her death ..."

"We are not going to discuss Mrs Bymeres or her death. I promised not to do so, and you must stick to my bargain because it was on that basis that we agreed to meet tonight."

"You really do want to forget her for the moment?"

"I like my Sunday nights off, too. And besides, before tomorrow is out, I'm sure you will have had enough of me talking about your friend. Because the talking will go on, you know. The probing, the questions, the insinuations, the misinterpretations, the anger, the frustration and the fear that go to make up a police investigation of this kind."

"I don't think I shall mind it nearly so much now you've told me."

"My dear Wanda, I haven't told you the half of it. People really get hurt when this sort of thing goes on, and you could be one of those who suffer."

"Thank you for calling me by my name, at least. It humanises it a little."

"You don't mind?"

"I have never ever spent an evening with a man of my own generation whom I have addressed as mister throughout. And your name, George, suits you. I know it means farmer, but a farmer's a fine calling. It provides the staff of life, after all."

"Thank you. Let me get you another drink."

She refused. When he asked her why, she said that she had decided to return home.

"So soon?"

She laughed. "There was a great deal of brandy in that Horse's Neck, and I've to drive home. It ill becomes a senior police officer to encourage a girl to drink and drive."

"That's not the reason." The liquor had not touched her. Of that he was sure.

She didn't reply.

"I see there's a garden at the back, and a small stream. Come and stroll it off."

Without a word she got to her feet and picked up her bag. As he followed her from the bar, she said: "There were some baby ducks on it last year."

It was inconsequential. He corrected her: "Duckling", and then cursed himself for being so pedantic.

"Baby ducks," she repeated. "Duckling is a word that only appears on menus nowadays."

They crossed the little lawn and came to the more tufted area of grass beside the stream. Wanda was clasping a bag in one hand and holding her skirt just off the ground with the other. The restriction made balancing difficult on high heels. He took her elbow to steady her. They moved slowly on in silence. The sky was darkening off, but nightfall was only apparent in the distance. Close at hand it was still light: comfortable, warm twilight. No word passed, but Masters could sense she was momentarily at peace as much as he was. This was a golden moment when people care: care for each other and tranquillity and beauty in all things. It was both a shock and a pleasure to him to know that she should care. As if to emphasise the realisation and to show he was included in her world, she passed the little bag over to the hand that grasped her skirt, and took his steadying hand in hers. They wandered along until a post and rail fence blocked their path. A horse in the field beyond munched noisily on, as if he accepted their presence but recognised in them nobody to disturb his activity. Masters, as unsure of himself as any youth at this juncture, tried to analyse his feelings towards her. He was greatly attracted. He didn't try to hide that from himself, but lurking at the back of his mind was the thought that the only attractive women he ever met in the course of his work were those connected—no matter how distantly—with crime. Sometimes as witnesses, often as suspicious characters. Like Wanda. Not for some years now had any woman affected him as this one did, and she ... well, she was under suspicion of being a murderess. No matter how hard he sought to dismiss the fact, he was too good a policeman to forget it entirely, even at a moment like this. And besides, she was another man's mistress. The thought pulled him up short. Caused him to break the spell.

"Where is Dr Bymeres tonight?"

Startled, she replied: "I don't know. Why do you ask?"

"Because," he answered gruffly, "if I were in his shoes I should want to be by your side tonight to ... to comfort you."

She said quietly. "I think we both thought that it would be wrong somehow. In the circumstances."

"In this day and age?"

"Does this day and age cater for, or set a fashion of behaviour for, such a bizarre situation?"

"I don't know. But whatever the reason, I'm pleased he is not with you."

She smiled. "That's a compliment isn't it?"

"It is. It's not pleasure at Bymeres' delicacy of feeling but

103

at my luck in your being free to be with me."

She gave his hand a squeeze. "You're nice to be with. Really reassuring. Now, I should like to go home."

As they returned to the inn he asked to be allowed to drive her home. The walk back to the Four-Fingered Hand from the cottage would, he assured her, be nothing to him. But she forbade it so firmly as to cause him not to insist, but so gently as to leave him in no doubt that had things been different, she would have wanted him with her.

After he had watched her tail lights disappear round the corner of the road leading to Little Munny, Masters sought out Green and Hill. As he had expected, he found them in one of the now almost deserted bars.

"You look as if you could do with a drink," said Green.

With a shock, Masters realised he had had nothing since dinner but the one Horse's Neck. "What's the bitter like?"

"Passable. A pint?"

When the drink came, Hill asked: "How did it go, chief?"

"Would you accept the simple answer—and all that it implies—that I think she is a charming woman?"

For a moment they both stared at him, then Green said: "Like that, is it?"

"Enough like that for me to ask you if you will be good enough to question her tomorrow in my place. If I were to do it I might not be truly objective."

Green seemed pleased. "I can put her through the hoop if needs be?"

"It'll be your session. There are one or two points I'd like you to clarify for me, in addition to whatever else you may ask on your own behalf."

"Okay. Such as?"

Masters spent a few minutes briefing Green. When he had finished, Hill asked: "What will you be doing, chief?"

"I thought you and I might drop the DI at Pilgrim's Cottage and then go on to see Bymeres. We'll be back later in the day of course to hear what the DI has learned at the cottage and to co-ordinate whatever has to be done next."

"Fair enough, chief. If you'd like another, I think there's just enough time to get one in before they shut the bar."

Chapter 7

IT WAS ONE of those bright mornings that seem so clean and unused because the world has been wrapped in mist and untouched by human hand until the sun has managed to tear away the wrapping and leave the pristine product exposed to view. The warmth of the sun, working like a slow furnace in a perfume house, had, in drying up the dew, driven off some of the essential oils of the aromatic plants—rose petals, wild thyme, hedgerow blossom, mint and scented stock—making of the light morning air a fragrant bouquet that appealed to senses other than simply that of smell. It even appealed to Green as he crunched his way up the gravel path to Pilgrim's Cottage. His step, though still heavy, was nonetheless lighter than usual. He half-whistled, half-hissed a little tune through lips held wide rather than pursed.

He was feeling more pleased with himself than he had done for some weeks. He got the impression that he was being better accepted by Masters than ever before, and he was speculating on his chances of being kept on in the team. He'd asked to leave it often enough in the past, but now the time had come to go he was realising that there were worse jobs. In fact, and this came as a bit of a shock to him, he now knew he would like to stay. Memory was one of Green's greatest assets, and nostalgia is closely allied to memory. So Green was recalling some of the team's sweet triumphs. Like all memories, his was skating over the bad bits and dredging up only the more pleasant ones.

It was just after half past nine. Masters and Hill had dropped him at the gate and had then gone on, hoping to reach Bymeres after he had finished morning surgery. Mrs Mace, Masters had guessed, would be up and about long before that time, so Green's call was not likely to be too inopportune.

So Green was approaching the cottage. He noted that all the windows and the back door were open. Somewhere within the house a radio was gently playing a Third programme Bach concert. He saw that a low table and two deck chairs had been put on the lawn. Mrs Mace was preparing for her interview with Masters? Green wondered how disappointed she would be that he, Green, had arrived in the superintendent's place.

As he neared the house, Wanda came out of the garage, carrying a large, red plastic base for a sun umbrella.

"Good morning, ma'am."

"Good morning, Mr Green. It's such a lovely day, I thought I'd put up the sunshade and sit in the garden."

"Can I help?"

"Would you? This needs filling with water. When it's full it's awfully heavy. I usually put it where I want it and then run the hose out to fill it, but if you could carry it...."

Green took it from her and went over to the outside tap. Wanda herself went back into the garage for the umbrella. They erected it on the lawn and moved the two chairs to take advantage of its shade.

"Thank you, Mr Green. Would you like some coffee? We could have it out here."

"Thank you."

"A quarter to ten isn't too early for you?"

"Not at all."

Green sat in one of the deck chairs after Wanda had gone indoors for the tray. She was courtesy itself, but it was plain to see she was disappointed at Masters' absence. He took off his jacket and hung it over the back of the chair and then, as an afterthought, removed his braces and took in the side tighteners on his trousers. When she returned, he said: "I suppose you were expecting the superintendent."

Surprisingly she answered: "Not really. I was definitely expecting a visit from one of you, but I felt sure, somehow, that Mr Masters wouldn't come himself."

"Fine. I thought he had told you that he would be here himself."

"Oh, he did. Do you like it white, Mr Green, or with just a touch of milk? No, I felt that after we had met last night he wouldn't come this morning."

"He'll be here later." Green took the cup of coffee and helped himself to sugar. Wanda had surprised him. She had not expected Masters, and Green could guess why. Masters had, despite all the talk, become too involved with this girl. He had said as much the night before. But it now seemed to Green that Wanda had become emotionally involved with Masters to the point where she could judge what actions the superintendent would take as a result of the relationship. In other words, Green told himself, the feeling's mutual between them. Being a romantic, Green felt vaguely pleased; and being a realist, he told himself that if he played his cards right here he could do himself a bit of good. It wasn't too far-fetched to suppose that this Wanda bird would have something to say to Masters about this interview, and if whatever she said was favourable to Green. . . .

His thoughts were interrupted by Wanda.

"Where is the superintendent?"

"He and Hill have gone to see Dr Bymeres."

"To see David?" She seemed puzzled by the news.

"Well now, Mrs Mace, he's the most important character in the case, you might say. After Mrs Bymeres, that is. It's always the near relatives, you know. We always look very closely at them—husbands in particular. Most sudden deaths" —he nearly said murders—"are domestic affairs"—he nearly said crimes—"you know." Having got this off his chest, Green took a gulp at the coffee. He felt rather pleased that he'd avoided two pitfalls more or less adroitly.

"But David wasn't even here when Daphne died."

Green looked straight at her. "Now look, Mrs Mace, there's been a sudden death. The doctors aren't satisfied, so we have to try and sort it out. You know that."

She nodded.

"So whatever happens," continued Green, "we've got to put a label on it sooner or later. Death from natural causes, suicide, death by misadventure or murder. We don't know the answer, but whichever it is, the husband is, to begin with at any rate, the person of prime interest to us because he's the one who can tell us most about his wife and, if there's been a crime, he's statistically the likeliest suspect. An' that's why the Super, being the boss man, has gone to see the doc himself."

"Am I under suspicion, too, that I merit the attention of the second in the team?"

Green put his cup down. "Now, you don't want me to answer that. You're a very intelligent woman. Mrs Bymeres died suddenly in your home and you're her husband's mistress."

"Put like that it sounds dreadful."

"Is there any other way of putting it?"

"In so few words, no. But if discussed less baldly, it might sound a little less like a two line plot for a TV serial."

"Right. So let's discuss it less baldly."

"We talked about it a lot yesterday."

"That was only clearing the ground, ma'am. We didn't arrive on the scene until late in the afternoon. I think we all understood that the Super and I were only clueing ourselves up from you and the two doctors who called. Getting ourselves into the sort of situation where we could start asking questions that mean something."

"I see. I wouldn't have thought there was still all that much to ask."

"Shall we see?" Green finished his coffee, declined a second cup and took out a new packet of Kensitas. He offered them to her silently and provided the match to light both cigarettes. When they were both leaning back, he asked: "What did you have to eat for dinner Friday night?"

"To see if Daphne could have got food poisoning? That's impossible. There were four of us besides her and we're all all right. She had nothing that we others didn't have. At the table, I mean."

"I'm sure everything you provided was perfectly clean and fresh, but I'd still like to know your menu."

"We started with a cold consommé, made with nothing

more harmful than the best known yeast extract on the market and beef broth—oh, and it had an onion in it and seasoning, of course."

"Very nice, too, for starters on a hot night. I bet everybody scoffed it."

"They were most complimentary about it."

"I'm sure. Go on, please. What next?"

"Pâté. I made it myself. I had the plates ready with a helping of pâté, a lettuce leaf and a ring of tomato on each. I served it with fingers of toast, of course."

"Was it liver pâté, or game?"

"Game. I couldn't make liver pâté, though it would have been easier. The only game at this time of the year is frozen."

"Why couldn't you use liver?"

"Because we were having liver and bacon as the main course. With onions and mushrooms."

"Potatoes?"

"Oh yés. I was forgetting. Duchesse potatoes and young broad beans served whole in their pods, with a plain white sauce."

Green stubbed his cigarette.

"You know, Mrs Mace, I'm getting the impression as you talk, when you use phrases like 'I couldn't make liver pâté though it would have been easier', that this menu was being specially prepared from a laid-down list from which you didn't want to stray."

"No list. The menu was entirely my own idea."

"I see. Please go on. No. Wait a moment! Plain white sauce? Not cheese sauce?"

"No. Plain or parsley but not cheese. That would have blanketed the flavour. But why all this insistence on cheese? I was asked if I'd served cheese by Dr Spiller yesterday morning."

"Naturally. Cheese reacts with some drugs."

"I've heard something about that, but I assure you there was no cheese in any of the cooking on Friday night and I didn't bring any to the table."

"Why not? I mean, most people offer cheese at the end

110

of a dinner party, don't they? Not that my missus ever gives dinner parties, but when there's anybody comes in for a meal she offers mousetrap in case anybody has any little holes to fill up."

"I didn't think it was necessary."

"Nobody suggested you shouldn't?"

"Mr Green, nobody suggested anything to me about my dinner party. I planned it myself, and I did the work myself, and nobody but me knew what the courses were going to be."

"Understood, Mrs Mace. What came after the liver and bacon?"

"Lemon mousse—my own make—and coffee."

"Sounds all right to me. I'd have liked a glass or two of vino with it, though."

"Sorry, I forgot. We had chianti, as it went with both game and liver."

Green grimaced. "Some of these chiantis can be a bit rough."

"I suppose so. Like most wines. I've had champagne that wasn't potable."

"Ah, well, it just goes to show. Mrs Bymeres ate hearty did she? Everything?"

"She ate hearty and she drank hearty. Too much so, some of us thought. Nobody seemed surprised when she complained of a headache."

"Because of her appetite?"

"Yes. Why else?"

"That would be the case with your visitors, but I wondered if you'd been warned by her husband that she was prone to headaches?"

"Yes, I was. And I could see why she got them."

"That's why you didn't do anything for her headache."

"I offered, but Daphne refused, so I left her to it. I know it sounds callous now, but at the time it seemed reasonable to me. One doesn't usually make a fuss over a headache, especially one which apparently comes quite frequently."

"And when all help is refused?"

111

"That's right. If I hadn't had other guests present...."

"I get you, Mrs Mace. Your actions seem reasonable enough to me."

"Thank you."

There was a little silence between them. But the garden was alive with sound and movement. The drone of a visiting bee nosey-parkering among the flowers. Birds so busy alighting and looking that they seemed to be taking the day off from work but without any clear idea of how best to use their time. A grey squirrel emulated the Grand Old Duke of York on the trunk of a tall tree nearby, making believe he had ten thousand men. Across the road, in the garden of one of the new bungalows, a small dog barked at every movement, whether of man or beast. But it was all background. Nothing obtruded. To those who didn't listen closely it would have been a silent forenoon. For a moment, Green watched Wanda. Her glorious head was back in the chair, but her hands betrayed a slight nervousness. One rosy-bloomed forefinger tapped a silent rhythm on the wood of the deck-chair arm.

"Mrs Mace," said Green, spoiling the idyll, "I'm sorry to have to harp on this business of your menu...."

"You still think there was something wrong with the food, don't you?" She sat forward as she spoke.

"I'm convinced that all the ingredients were sweet enough."

"What then?"

"I said a few minutes ago that you had given me the impression you were following a very definite plan in choosing your dishes. You said I was mistaken. But the impression persists."

"Do you usually pick up nuances so easily?"

"If that means what I think it does, I suppose the answer is yes, because in our game you hear so many stories that practice makes you read between the lines. And that's what you'd call a mixed metaphor, I suppose."

"Nevertheless I understand your meaning well enough. I repeat, I was not following a plan, but I had a very definite object in view when I decided what to put on for dinner."

112

Green was slightly startled. He wondered whether he should caution her to be careful. A definite object in view! Daphne Bymeres' death, by any chance? If she was going to spill the beans here and now....

She interrupted his thought flow. "What I set out to do, Inspector, was to combine in one meal all the dishes that I knew David Bymeres liked best. It was to be a surprise for him. But he wasn't there to enjoy it."

Green felt flummoxed. "You say all the dishes had been chosen with Dr Bymeres in mind, but he knew nothing about them?"

"Not a thing."

"Could he have guessed?"

"I don't think so. Everything except the liver and bacon was cold, you see. It was all prepared and hidden away in the pantry, under covers, before he arrived. He might have smelled the liver cooking, but I don't think so, because I get very few cooking smells in the house, and those there were on Friday night would be masked by the onions, which could be served with almost anything."

Green selected another Kensitas.

"You definitely did not ask Dr Bymeres what he would like for dinner—if it was to be in his honour, as it were?"

"I definitely never mentioned it to him."

"Right." He lit the cigarette. "Now though your menu sounds very good and very simple, there are one or two things that strike me as rather funny about it."

"Oh?"

"We've dealt with no cheese at the end, so we'll skip that one. But what about whole broad beans? I've never heard of anybody eating them in their pods before. So I reckon that's unusual, and anything unusual is worth enquiring about."

"Mr Green." She got to her feet and stacked the coffee things on the tray, preparatory to taking them indoors. "You have assured me, or re-assured me would be more accurate, that all the food I provided was wholesome. Yet, even after that admission, you are enquiring into it as though it could

113

be responsible for Daphne's death. I think I am entitled to know why."

"Sit down again. Please!" said Green. "You're an intelligent woman. It sticks out a mile. But you're forgetting something."

She sat down. "What?"

"Forgetting or overlooking the fact that we, too, have a modicum of intelligence."

"Oh, no!"

"You're assuming that my questions are pointless."

"No, I'm not."

"Then you are well aware that they have reason behind them?"

"I suppose I could admit that."

Green put his head on one side and regarded her as if considering what next to say. Then he went on: "Look, love, if you're ready to admit there's a reason for what I'm asking you, why try to head me off?"

"I don't really know."

"Shall I take it that you merely find the questions a bit irritating—perhaps boring?"

"I'd better settle for that, I suppose, but to be honest, it's because I find them frightening."

"Why?"

"Fear of the unknown, I suppose, because I can't see where they are heading. When I admit that they must have point, otherwise I presume you would not be asking them, I must also confess that I can't see that point. For me that's rather frightening—in these particular circumstances."

"Well now, ma'am that's about the best answer you could give from your point of view."

"It's not a particularly illuminating one or a coherent one if it comes to that."

"Maybe not, but you see I could have interpreted your interruptions quite differently if you hadn't told me you were just frightened and nothing more."

"I see. What interpretation?"

"Isn't it obvious? A suspicious chap like me could jump to

114

the conclusion that you knew exactly where I was heading and you were trying to steer me away from what was dangerous ground for you."

Her look of surprised outrage pleased him. He was happy, too, that she did not start to expostulate. He would have thought very different thoughts had she started to protest too much. Instead she smiled wryly. "At least you admit to being a suspicious man."

"That's right." He became avuncular. "Your best bet, love, is to trust us. We're not getting at you, you know—even if we do irritate you a bit. We're sorting a problem. Now it may be that you don't think there's any problem to sort. But I'd like to bet when something funny has happened in the past which hasn't concerned you personally, you've said to somebody: 'What are the police doing about it?' or 'The police should be looking into that, not hounding innocent motorists'. Come on now, admit it. Everybody says it at some time."

She smiled. "I have."

"Right. So what's the point in getting irritated when we do start looking into things? Let's get back to those beans. How often have you eaten broad beans in their pods?"

"Never—before Friday night, that is."

It was Green's turn to look surprised. "Never? Then what on earth possessed you to dish 'em up on Friday?"

"I told you. David likes them."

Green shook his head. "It won't do, love."

"What on earth do you mean?"

"How often have you fed Dr Bymeres? I mean, he was a pretty frequent visitor here. You didn't always send him away hungry, did you?"

"Of course not. I've prepared meals for us scores of times."

"But never broad beans in their pods."

"No."

"Why not, if they're such a great favourite of his?"

"Because I didn't know he liked them until last week, otherwise I might have cooked them before."

"Ah!" Green leaned back, lips pursed. Her face was quite serene, except for just a little frown of puzzlement. "Now

115

tell me, Mrs Mace, how did you get to know that he liked them? Did he just up and say so, or what?"

"The answer is quite simple, Inspector. I was having lunch with him last Monday and the beans were on the menu. He ordered them for himself. Because I'd never encountered them before, I remarked on them. He told me he doted on them, so when I came to plan dinner on Friday—it being planned in his honour, as it were—I included them in my menu. He'd told me they should never be served with cheese sauce, so I knew how to prepare them. I thought they would please him and be a novelty for the rest of us."

"That sounds very reasonable to me, except for one thing. You and he must have eaten out together quite a lot...."

"I know what you're going to say. I should have come across his liking for beans before last Monday. But you're wrong in assuming that David and I ate out very often. We didn't. For several reasons. Our little affair was conducted over a distance of twelve miles. David could only get out to see me at times which wouldn't arouse Daphne's suspicions. For an afternoon perhaps, when he would otherwise have been playing golf; or for an hour or two in a day when his list of calls wasn't too heavy. Such meetings gave us little opportunity to book tables and flog off to restaurants, besides which, we were a *little* circumspect, you know. David wasn't too happy when eating out lest somebody who knew him and Daphne should see us. Doctors have to be a bit more careful than most people...."

"I see...."

"Please let me finish, Mr Green. The last thing I want to add is that there is a very short season for those young beans. We should have had to have gone out during those few weeks, and hit upon a restaurant that served them for me to have learned of his liking for them."

"All very logical," said Green. "But if you didn't normally go out to restaurants, why have lunch with him in one last Monday? What was so special about last Monday?"

"Not a lot, really, but I hadn't been seeing quite so much of David in the last six or eight weeks. I think the doctors

116

in the practice were starting to take their summer holidays and those left behind had to share the work."

"That's what he told you, is it?"

"Yes. Why do you ask?"

"You said you *thought* that was the reason. I'm only trying to get my facts solid. It seems a perfectly logical reason. I assure you I wasn't suggesting he was going off you, Mrs Mace. No man would be that daft."

"A compliment. Mr Green, how gallant!"

Green blushed. "Last Monday!" he grunted, to remind her that she was explaining the reason for the luncheon meeting.

"Oh, yes! It was getting difficult for David to find the time to get out here, but he thought we ought to meet to discuss Daphne's visit. So he killed two birds with one stone, as it were. He invited me to lunch in a delightful little pub called the Bramblebush, which is about eight miles from here, and four miles from his surgery. We had our little luncheon party and discussed Daphne, and then I went on from there to call on Daphne and persuaded her to come. David had a clinic that afternoon, but he was only four miles away, so he could make it quite easily, whereas coming out here would have been quite a chore in his lunch break."

"I see. And this pub served whole broad beans."

"Regularly, in season, I think. At any rate David had had them before. He asked the waiter if they were still on the list of vegetables."

"And that's how you first heard of them and got to know he had a weakness for them. That's cleared that point up. But I'm surprised that, if Dr Bymeres recommended them so highly, you didn't try them yourself there and then."

"I tested just one and liked it. I would have ordered them for myself if I'd been having liver and bacon like him, but I'd ordered crab salad, so I didn't have hot vegetables."

Green spoke slowly. "Liver and bacon, you say? He must be a devil for liver and bacon. How often did you have to lob that up for him?"

"I don't believe I ever did."

117

"But if he liked it so much that you prepared it specially for dinner on Friday...?"

"I didn't know he liked it as much as he said he did last Monday. Please don't make a thing of it all. When we had lunch, he chose the things he liked best on the menu. When I decided to have my little dinner party, as it was especially for him, I thought I couldn't please him more than by repeating the menu. I added the game pâté, because he was a bit undecided on Monday as to whether he should choose that or liver. There's no great mystery to it, and as far as I can see, nothing sinister, either."

"At any rate," replied Green, "it clears up any last points —as to why you chose chianti as the wine with dinner. I was really surprised by that, as I wouldn't have thought it a woman's wine, but I suppose the doctor drank it last Monday."

"That's so. Privately, I agree with you, but David praised its roughness and bite so much that I thought it must have some property I'd missed on the few occasions when I'd tried it, so I bought the best one I could for Friday night, and it seemed to go down well enough."

Green offered her another cigarette. As he drew slowly on his own, he said. "Now just let me get this straight, then I reckon we could have that other cup of coffee you mentioned. The menu on Friday night was exactly the same as that chosen by Dr Bymeres last Monday."

"Except for the pâté which I put in."

"But which he had havered over?"

"Yes. And of course, I added the lemon mousse."

"You didn't have a sweet last Monday?"

"No, there wasn't time. But I always do have lemon mousse at dinner parties. It's the only really pretty sweet I'm any good at making properly."

"And as you were making it in his honour, I suppose you knew the doc would like it."

"He dotes on it. It's got Kirsch in it. He didn't know what there was going to be for dinner, but if you'd asked him, I bet he would have sworn he would get lemon mousse for sweet. He knows it's the only thing I make well among the things one would want to put on for dinner. I can make rice puddings and such like well enough, but they're not dinner party dishes."

"I'm sure you can. Now, can I help with the coffee?"

"No. Sit still. It won't take me a moment."

Green was in a mental quandary. He'd conducted the interview strictly according to the brief given him by Masters. He ought to have guessed that questions concerning the strange facets of the dinner party that Masters had told him to ask would lead to information which would warrant investigation over and above the bounds of the brief. Not that he was in any way worried about taking matters into his own hands and conducting a further session of questioning following his own line. He was free to use his initiative, but he wasn't too sure that the time was right for letting Wanda know how Daphne died. As yet she seemed to be in the dark about this. If she wasn't she was a clever actress. But ought he to keep a trick up his sleeve to give Masters the benefit of surprise should he need it later? Normally Green might not have had this mental debate, but he was very anxious at the moment not to put a foot wrong. He was still undecided when Wanda reappeared with the tray. He supposed he would have to play it as it came.

"Did you tell Dr Bymeres what a treat he'd missed when he was here yesterday?"

"There didn't seem to be time. And besides, discussing a menu would seem to be a trivial matter just after somebody has died rather mysteriously."

"I suppose so." Green helped himself to sugar. "Her death —or the cause of it—is still a mystery to you, Mrs Mace?"

"I've thought and thought about it, but I can see no answer."

"The doctor didn't pass an opinion while he was with you yesterday or Saturday?"

"David? No. I asked him, naturally, but he said we would have to wait for the pathologist's report."

119

"Just like that? No guesses at all, even though he is a doctor?"

"I think he refused to speculate in my presence in order to spare my feelings. He said we ought to avoid the subject and ... well, so we did."

"For two whole days? He was here on Saturday quite early in the morning and yesterday till after we arrived, remember."

"Quite honestly, there wasn't a moment. There were police and doctors milling round and asking questions all Saturday. David was busy with them more than I was, but I seemed to be making everlasting cups of tea. It was after two o'clock before I could get David and myself a biscuit and cheese for lunch. We tried to eat, but neither of us had any appetite. Then David had to go. I should think he had a lot to do and people to see. He came back yesterday just before lunch, and we'd barely sat down to it before the local inspector arrived to tell us Scotland Yard had been called in. David wanted to know what the pathologist's report had said, but the inspector said it wasn't ready yet. That got David's back up and he and the inspector got a bit short with each other. Then in no time at all, you arrived. David only waited a short time after that before he went."

"Did he seem at all worried?"

"What about?"

"The police enquiry."

"No. Just the reverse. I think he was sorry about Daphne's death, of course, although he told me it was in many ways a great relief to him. But he seemed totally unconcerned about the police activity, and kept telling me to forget it, too."

"Surely he couldn't just ignore the police in the house and expect you to do the same?"

"I assure you that was his attitude. He said they were on a wild goose chase started by Spiller who should have known better than to start it, and he was damned if he was going to join in their little games."

"He was angry?"

"No. Amused, I'd say. I was surprised at how cheerful he was. I think it was his attitude that kept me on an even keel."

120

"Obviously a good man under pressure."

"He appears to be. Certainly he's a very good doctor."

"I'm sure he is."

"You said that as if you didn't believe me."

Green put his cup down. "Well now, Mrs Mace, how good a doctor is one who doesn't know that certain foods are lethal with certain drugs?"

"I don't think I understand."

"Mrs Bymeres was on medicines which are incompatible with a substance called tyramine which is found in cheese...."

"But Daphne didn't eat any cheese."

He ignored the interruption. "In cheese, and certain other foods and drinks, the chief of which are yeast extract, game, liver, whole broad beans, citrus fruits and chianti."

He was watching her closely as he spelled out the list. He saw the colour drain from her face and her body stiffen in the chair. Her gaze, horrified, was on him. As he finished, one lovely hand came up to her mouth.

"Oh, my God!" she whispered. "It was me! I killed her."

Chapter 8

MASTERS LOCATED THE group surgery at a few minutes past ten. The door was still unlocked, so he walked straight in. The general waiting room was almost empty. Two old men sat mumbling in one corner. A mother with a placid child, too pale to be healthy, sat resignedly in the middle of the row of chairs against the near wall. A young man in disreputable jeans and washed-out T shirt sat reading an old copy of *Motor*, chewing gum, and nursing what appeared to be a damaged hand swathed in bandages no longer white. None of these paid any attention to the huge newcomer. A glass window opposite the door, however, slid open, and a woman's hand appeared.

"Can I help you?"

"Are you, by any chance, Miss Hector?"

"I am. Who are you? A representative?"

"In a way. I'm a representative of the law, if you don't object to the old way of describing us."

"A policeman?"

"Detective Superintendent Masters of Scotland Yard, ma'am. Sergeant Hill, my assistant, will be here in a moment."

It seemed that all conversations at the window were conducted in whispers. Certainly nobody appeared to have overheard Masters' introduction of himself.

"What can I do for you?"

"I wish to see Dr Bymeres when he's free. On official business."

"I see. Concerning the death of his wife, I suppose?"

"It is official, ma'am, and consequently confidential."

Miss Hector, Masters guessed, was forty plus. Her hair was grey, but extremely neatly and softly done. Her face was round and unwrinkled, but it lacked the pleasant mouth line and the humour in the eyes that one would have hoped for in a motherly woman of like mien. She looked, not hard exactly, but too businesslike for comfort. Probably her job as administrator or secretary of this practice had robbed her of the softness one might have expected. He could see one of her hands. It was that of a woman who might have to dust a bachelor flat, but who had never had to run a house for husbands and kids. She wore a light grey suit and a white blouse tied at the neck. His remark about the confidentiality of his call did not appear to please her.

"I know everything that goes on in this practice."

"Then you will know whether Dr Bymeres is free now," said Masters blandly. He felt affronted by Miss Hector. He was sufficient of a male chauvinist pig to resent women who, having been granted the looks and everything else necessary to make them a pleasure to meet, should deliberately adopt an attitude of prying aloofness which irritated. He wondered how many patients' days had been ruined by an encounter with Miss Hector. A little power was a dangerous thing in some people.

"He is with his last patient now. I will ring and ask him if he has time to see you before rounds."

"Please don't do that. Just tell him I'm here to see him. I'm sure he wouldn't thank you for suggesting a course of action which, if taken, might result in him wasting quite a long time in a police station—with his rounds still to do."

"That sounds to me suspiciously like police pressure."

"That's exactly what it is, ma'am. Pressure on you to do as you are requested and not to think up alternative courses of action which I am empowered to interpret as impeding me in the course of my duty. Ah! Here's my sergeant. Sergeant, this is Miss Hector. See that she informs Dr Bymeres that I will see him in his consulting room in about three minutes."

"Right, chief."

"I'll be back. I left my tobacco in the car."

"About forty yards along on this side, chief. Here's the key."

*   *   *

123

The surgery was not tailor-made for the job. The premises had at one time been a largish lock-up shop, with house above and behind. The shop was now the waiting room. Half the store behind it was Miss Hector's province. The other half was a central filing area. Two doctors had small surgeries in what remained of the ground floor. The other doctors were upstairs. On the landing was a communal weighing machine and other items of equipment which, it seemed, need not be installed singly in every consulting room.

Bymeres, as one of the middle-piece partners, had a back room. Not large, but at least not one of the bigger rooms divided. His small desk was against the wall to the left as one entered the room. The patients' chair, at the end of the desk and behind the door was very close to the doctor's own, but Masters noticed that it faced the window so that Bymeres could get a full view of whoever was visiting him. Masters, after entering and introducing himself and Hill, and being invited to take a seat, moved the chair so that Bymeres had to swing half round away from the desk to face him. Hill took the second upright chair.

Masters' immediate impression of Bymeres was that he was natty. Not a big man, though well built, he was too neat even for the fastidious Masters, whose vanity drove him to clothe himself in Savile Row. Bymeres had on a blue pin stripe suit and a blue figured shirt, the collar of which was just too long as to the points, and the cuffs just too prominent, as if needed to display cuff links made from greeny-blue nacre. The knot of the tie was halfway to Carnaby Street. The face was smooth, well rounded, perfectly shaved and just as perfectly dusted to remove soap-shine. The darkish-fair hair was cut commendably short. The sideboards were scarcely there, but perfectly edged. The front of the hair was, however, swept up from the forehead and brought back down into the centre of the crown in a coif that depended on some dressing or fixative to hold it in place, as the comb-striation marks plainly showed. Natty! Masters told himself privately not to be too censorious, as his attitude might well be coloured by the fact that even if this man wasn't a villain, at least he had been guilty of bedding Wanda Mace, and the thought was distasteful in the extreme.

"I'd like to say how sorry I am about Mrs Bymeres, doctor."

"Thank you."

"You were aware that I had been called in, even though we didn't meet yesterday afternoon. What I'd like now is a chat so that I can get the background of this business."

"The police seem to be determined to make something of my wife's death. I'm the next of kin. That means I'm the prime suspect, I suppose." The voice was deprecating, carefully controlled and yet held a hint of mockery. Masters was in no mood to be needled by this man. If he wanted to play it like some smart-alec tough, fair enough. Masters couldn't care less.

"Suspect? Of what ought we to be suspicious, doctor?"

"You suspect me of killing my wife." It was said with the merest of grins playing round the lips.

"You're going a little too fast for me, sir. I didn't even know that your wife had been killed. Dead, yes. But killed? That would mean murdered."

"Oh, come now, Superintendent! You're from the Yard. Even I know you're one of the most famous of the murder-squad buffs."

Hill interrupted.

"I think, doctor, you haven't quite appreciated Superintendent Masters' point."

"I have, Sergeant. I'm not that naïve."

"Even the least naïve among us can jump to wrong conclusions, sir. Mrs Bymeres died in her bed on Friday night. Her death was, apparently, completely unexpected. But sudden death isn't all that uncommon as you, being a doctor, will know. In such cases, it's entirely up to you medics. You're either satisfied as to the cause of death, or you're not satisfied. If you're not, you call us in. But even we have to rely on you doctors to give us the cause and reason. Without your information we can't say whether there's just been a natural death or an unnatural one. But we've got to try and find out.

What I'm saying is, that your lot present us with the problem, but don't say what it is. So when the chief hears you talk of murder, he's more than interested."

"You are trying to cod me, Sergeant, that you are here simply to establish how she died."

"Initially, yes, sir. It's only if we reckon that somebody killed her that we'll start treating it as murder."

"Rubbish. The two enquiries go hand in hand."

"Naturally they do—sometimes," said Masters. "I've known the time when I've been obliged to treat a death as murder in order to establish that it wasn't. The cart before the horse, as it were. But in this case, doctor, Mrs Bymeres did not die from overt violence or ascertainable poisoning, but from what we must term clinical causes—intracranial haemorrhage and cardiac arrest—both of which occur frequently in natural deaths. So, we've got to decide whether natural causes are natural or unnatural in this case, and we're far from arriving at a conclusion, I assure you."

"You've made your point."

"Have I? I'm pleased about that because I have sometimes been accused of going a little too fast, without explaining detail."

"Not this time. But this is the time—after surgery—when we have coffee. Would you like some?"

"Yes, please."

Bymeres spoke into an intercom. Then he turned back to Masters. "At least you don't seem afraid I shall poison you."

"You have a morbid sense of humour, doctor. If I suspected you of having poisoned Mrs Bymeres, our conversation would not be being conducted on your home ground but in a very bare and unpleasant interview room in a police station."

"Thank heaven for that reassurance."

"Do you mind if I smoke my pipe?"

"It's not usually done, to allow smoking in a consulting room, but we can stretch a point in your case. Perhaps the sergeant wouldn't mind opening the window." As Hill got to his feet, Bymeres stretched across and emptied an old enamelled kidney dish of pencils and rubbers and placed it on the corner of the desk nearest Masters.

"I am wary of the reassurance you have just given me, Superintendent."

Masters dropped the dead match in the kidney dish. "I gave you no reassurance, doctor. I stated a fact as I see it. No more, no less. It is no part of my job to give reassurances."

"I read it as a reassurance. Is it part of the play? To reassure me in the hope of catching me off guard?"

There was a tap at the door and a young woman came in with a tray of ready-poured coffee in a motley mixture of crockery.

"Thank you, Sonia."

"Miss Hector would like to know how long you'll be, doctor. She has your visits' list ready."

"Tell her not to worry, Sonia. The list can't be very long."

Sonia left. "She's our secretary-bird. Very fast on the typewriter but not very quick on the uptake."

Nor, thought Masters, in responding to the suggestive pleasantries of young Dr Bymeres. But he let it go and accepted the cup of wash handed to him.

"You are virtually accusing me of being less than frank with you, Dr Bymeres. No doubt, with your professional knowledge of psychiatry, you can provide motives, other than those I intend, for every word I say. But please use your knowledge on your own behalf. You are acting as though you are guilty of something or other."

"Correction! Acting as though I think you are convinced I am guilty of some unspecified crime. The difference is so appreciable as to be signficant even to you."

"I see." Masters struck another match and applied it to his pipe in an effort to get an even burn across the surface of the Warlock Flake. "Well now, to clear the air a little, and so that you shall not be in a position to accuse me of trying to catch you out," he paused and gave a few quick puffs, "let me say at the outset, and entirely to please you, that I consider you as a murder suspect, and Mrs Mace as another. Does that satisfy you?"

Bymeres had paled slightly, but he had lost none of his

127

bounce. "No, it does not, because you just said that you hadn't established murder."

"True." Masters wagged his pipe stem at Bymeres. "But you are running on a bit, doctor. You seem to have a nervous inability to stop your tongue running away with you. I don't want to take advantage of your attitude, because it may lead me astray. You see, I often encounter it. A lot of perfectly innocent people are nervous with police about—particularly in circumstances such as these."

The words were a blow to Bymeres' pride, as Masters had anticipated.

"I'm not nervous, dammit."

"No? That's fine. We have no need to worry, then. But it seemed to me you were evincing some of the signs of persecution mania. Didn't it seem so to you, Sergeant?"

"It did, chief. The doctor accused us of suspecting him and then invited us to do just that. And that gives us another problem, doesn't it?"

Bymeres glanced from one to the other. He seemed to have recovered his aplomb. The faint smirk of amusement had returned. "You two are like a couple of cross-talk comedians. What extra problem have I set you now?"

"Well, sir," continued Hill, "we've got to try and decide whether whatever you say springs from a sense of guilt or from sheer nervousness. I reckon that if you were to drink your coffee it might settle your nerves a bit."

Bymeres took up the cup and tasted the contents. "It really is the foulest muck they make here."

"You're one of the bosses," said Masters.

"I know. But you don't know Miss Hector, our resident dragon. A mere suggestion that the coffee might be improved would cause the sort of rumpus I prefer to avoid. But if ever you hear she's been quietly done away with, you won't have to look far for the culprit."

"I met her—and exchanged a few words. A lady of uncertain temper with an immense love of power was what I judged her to be."

"She is. But she's efficient, so we put up with her."

128

"Efficiency being at a premium these days?"

"Almost non-existent in most walks of life."

"There are many who would agree with you."

"Meaning you don't?"

"Oh, I do. But discussions on the subject are liable to become political, and I must avoid that. But to return to the business in hand. My enquiries so far tell me that Mrs Mace and your wife were friends of long standing. However, since your wife became neurotic, they have seen little of each other, and your wife rarely, if ever, visited Pilgrim's Cottage until this holiday came along. But you, doctor, visited the cottage regularly and, according to Mrs Mace, you and she have been lovers since Mrs Bymeres' illness started. Is that, in essence, correct?"

"Of course it is. If Wanda gave you the facts, why ask?"

"I was really doing you the favour of letting you know how much we know of your affairs, and giving you the opportunity of adding to them or of denying them."

"I suppose that information leads you to think that we ... Wanda and I ... conspired to kill Daphne."

"It's a thought. I agree that we seem to have a classic case of the eternal triangle which so often forms the basis for crime, but I have a feeling that such a simple solution would be just too easy in this case, and besides, I have no facts to support it. Rather the reverse if anything."

"What do you mean by that?"

"I cannot believe that two people as intelligent as you and and Mrs Mace would collaborate in so obvious a little plot as this eternal triangle would seem to present us with. I might be more ready to believe in the possibility had your affair with Mrs Mace been more clandestine. But you were neither of you at very great pains to hide it, and that doesn't seem to march very well with a lot of secret plotting and collusion."

"So you definitely rule out the possibility of Wanda and me collaborating to kill Daphne?"

"Shall we say for the moment? Definitely is rather finite, and I don't want to mislead you. But tell me, did you and Mrs Mace ever discuss marriage—one with another?"

"Hell's teeth! Of course not. I was married to Daphne. I could never have divorced her. No, Superintendent, I swear we neither of us ever mentioned it."

"I asked, because though you may consider it unthinkable for a doctor to divorce a sick wife, there was nothing to stop Mrs Bymeres divorcing you—were she to hear of your conduct with Mrs Mace. Or would the attendant scandal make such a step on her part unthinkable, too?"

"There would have been no scandal. Wanda Mace is not one of my patients, so though I might be cited for infidelity there would be no hint of unprofessional conduct."

"Now you are sure, doctor, that your relationship with Mrs Mace did not cause or exacerbate Mrs Bymeres' condition? I mean, chronic depression must be affected by events."

"My relationship with Wanda bégan after Daphne became a chronic neurotic. In fact it was her neurosis that caused the relationship, if you like. Nor did our friendship exacerbate Daphne's condition because she knew nothing about it."

"Perhaps not. But Mrs Bymeres might have suspected that you were being unfaithful. And that suspicion—even if not confirmed—could have affected her adversely. So did she, in fact, suspect you?"

"Well, yes, she did."

"She actually accused you of infidelity?"

"Yes."

"And you denied it?"

"No. I had no need to."

"Amazing! Why not?"

"Daphne accused me of running about with another woman. It was a bit of a shock, but I kept my head enough to realise that if she'd known it was Wanda, she'd have said so. She couldn't have resisted blurting it out."

"Go on."

"So when she accused me, I simply asked her who she thought I was running about with. And her answer was so ludicrous I just laughed. I'd no need to deny anything. I just laughed her suggestion out of court."

130

"How?"

"Because Daphne named Miss Hector, of all people. And the idea of Miss H and me ... well, I assure you I nurture no passion for her. So you see I neither denied nor confirmed Daphne's accusation, and I certainly never mentioned Wanda's name."

Hill said: "What you've just told us, doctor, seems to be borne out by the fact that Mrs Bymeres went to Pilgrim's Cottage last weekend. She wouldn't have gone to spend a holiday with her husband's mistress now, would she?"

Bymeres inclined his head towards Hill. "Thank you, Sergeant."

"Now we've mentioned the holiday," said Masters, "let's discuss that for a moment. First of all, whose idea was it that Mrs Bymeres should be invited to stay at the cottage?"

"Wanda's," said Bymeres quickly.

"You're absolutely sure of that?"

"It's her cottage, dammit, I can't invite guests there."

"Not directly, perhaps. But you can ask or suggest that somebody be invited."

"I honestly believe that you people could find three alternative meanings for the word yes. Is it important who invited Daphne? She was there."

Masters leaned over to tap the burnt top ash out of his pipe and then started to relight the dead tobacco. "It is important, Dr Bymeres, or could be, and you know it."

"Do I?"

"Furthermore, I cannot for the life of me believe that a sensitive woman would suddenly invite her lover's wife to stay without some prompting, unless she had a sinister purpose."

"You can believe what you like."

"I repeat, I cannot accept that Mrs Mace would, unprompted, invite your wife, unless there was a sinister motive."

"And I repeat, you can think what you like. The motive behind Wanda's gesture was far from sinister. It was to do me a good turn. She knew that I needed a break from

131

Daphne, which I wouldn't get by going on holiday, because I'd be expected to take Daphne with me. The only chance I could possibly have was if someone were to take Daphne off my hands for a good time. Wanda realised that if she were to offer, she would be doing me a good turn—and Daphne, too."

"And it wasn't your suggestion?"

"No."

"Then how did Mrs Mace know it was necessary?"

"It wasn't *necessary*."

"Desirable then. Had you been discussing it with her?"

"I may have mentioned it. But not that she should have Daphne. Merely that I would have to find a place where Daphne could go alone so that I could have a break."

"Come off it," said Hill.

"I beg your pardon?"

"You said a moment ago that if you went on holiday you'd have to take your wife with you. What's the difference between that and finding a hotel for your wife to go on holiday alone? She'd want you with her then. It's the same difference, in fact. I reckon you mentioned you were trying to do it and had had no luck—because you hadn't tried very hard—and Mrs Mace fell for it. As any woman would, in her position, seeing she was a friend of your wife and more than a bit pally with you."

Bymeres was growing angry. He faced Masters, his lips in a straight line and his eyebrows drawn down. "Now look here, I'm not prepared to have that sort of thing from the sergeant, from you, or anybody else. I give you an honest account, and your man here as good as tells me I'm lying."

"He certainly seems to think your story doesn't hold water," admitted Masters blandly. "And I can't say that I blame him. I, too, really believe that you used your privileged relationship with Mrs Mace to ensure—by indirect means—that your wife went there for this holiday."

"So?"

"So Mrs Mace was prompted into making the invitation."

"And I say no. Ask Wanda."

132

Masters forebore from telling Bymeres that Wanda had already admitted that the idea had been hers and hers alone. Superficially, perhaps, it had been. But Masters was not prepared to accept there had not been indirect pressure on Wanda to invite Daphne. So he started on a new tack after a suitable pause.

"I understand that you were to have stayed at Pilgrim's Cottage yourself over the weekend."

"On paper, yes."

"I think you'll agree that such an answer needs a little amplification, doctor."

"Of course it does. But in the present context even the most innocent of little ruses assumes sinister proportions. That's why I say that on paper I was to stay the weekend. But that was said for Daphne's benefit. Both Wanda and I knew different."

"Please be more explicit."

"Daphne wouldn't have agreed to the holiday if I hadn't promised to be with her as much as possible. That meant that I had to take her and stay with her on Friday to settle her in and generally acclimatise her to Pilgrim's Cottage. I knew that if Wanda were to come for her she wouldn't go; and if I were just to deliver her there with the intention of coming straight back she wouldn't have got out of the car. So she had to be told I would be staying. But that would have rendered the plan useless. The whole idea was for me to be free of Daphne for as long as possible, though obviously she couldn't be told that. Besides, Wanda and I had a few of the finer feelings left—we didn't really want to be there together with Daphne. So I arranged to have a bogus call put through at half past nine on Friday night, calling me back to see a patient."

"After which you wouldn't have returned?"

"No. We reckoned that once she was settled in and had had dinner, and passed one night at the cottage, Daphne would have accepted my absence."

"I see. So you had intended to stay for the dinner party...."

"I didn't know there was to be a party. Not until I saw the dining table laid just before I got the phone call. I was intending to stay until after the three of us had eaten."

"But you got a call before dinner—a genuine one."

"Yes. The best laid schemes...."

"A pity. Had you not been called away, your wife might not have died."

"I don't see how you can possibly say that. As I understand it she was alive and perfectly well—except for a headache—at the time I would have left to answer the bogus call."

"That is so. But you see, Dr Bymeres, your wife ate food at dinner that night that was incompatible with Dr Spiller's medication."

"You're joking. What does Spiller say was incompatible with the tranquillisers he was prescribing for Daphne? As far as I know, nothing is contra-indicated in the food line. Too much alcohol is a bad thing, of course, but Daphne wouldn't be tossing back double scotches."

Masters tapped out his pipe in the dish and spoke over the noise. "Are you telling me you didn't know what medication your wife was on, doctor?"

"Of course not. She was on Valium. Had been for months. I knew she was on it."

"She wasn't."

"Wasn't? Since when? I didn't interfere or ask too many questions because she was Spiller's patient, and he's the last chap I should want to imagine I was poking my nose in. But the last I knew of her drugs was that she was on Valium."

"You did not know she was on monoamine oxidase inhibitors?"

"M.A.O.I.s? No, I certainly didn't. When did he put her on those?"

"Quite recently."

"And I suppose she ate cheese on Friday night against his instructions. Is that it?"

"No cheese. And you're right, he did warn her against cheese. But he didn't warn her about a few more rare foods

134

like whole broad beans, game and chianti."

"Oh, my God! Was that what Wanda served up?"

"You didn't know what her menu was to be, doctor?"

"No. I swear to God I didn't know one single item of the menu. Wanda didn't tell me, and I didn't ask. I didn't ask afterwards, either." He looked at Masters. "There was no reason why I should have done. I thought Daphne was on Valium and could eat what she liked. I knew Wanda would never have served up any food that wasn't good."

Masters nodded and tamped a fresh bowlful of tobacco. Between sucks at the stem to see that it would still draw, he said: "That agrees with what I heard. I was told that the meal was to be a surprise for you. Mrs Mace was preparing a number of your favourite dishes and didn't want you to know what they were to be till they were set before you."

"Thank you for the confirmation," said Bymeres.

"You say that as though I were deliberately trying to misinterpret or disbelieve every word you utter."

"Aren't you?"

"I'm trying to weigh every word, certainly. But you've no idea how pleased I am to get nuggets of corroborated proof. They're the only things that help me. Like the scraps of gold left in a prospector's washing pan. I've got to be able to recognise them for what they are. Fool's gold may shine bright, but it's of no value to me."

"You're a funny bloke for a copper."

"You think I could make a name for myself on the halls?"

"I've no doubt you could. I meant that I should think you are out of the mainstream of policemen."

"I pride myself I am, but Hill would be better able to answer that question than me." He pocketed his tobacco and matches. "Thank you, Dr Bymeres, that's all for now. We'll let you get on with your visits."

"Wait a moment, Superintendent."

"There's something you wish to say, doctor?"

"This seems to be a most unsatisfactory end to an interview."

"Who for?"

"Me."

"Really? I would have said—and I speak from experience —that the most unsatisfactory end to any chat with me is when the interviewee is hauled off to durance vile there and then. You are free to come and go as you please."

"Don't give me that. I get the distinct impression that you will be visiting me again."

"Very likely."

"I want to know why. You agree I knew nothing of the food which Daphne ate, I wasn't even present when she ate it, and even if I had known she was on M.A.O.I.s I could have done nothing to prevent her eating the food since I didn't know what it was."

"That seems to be a logical summing up, doctor."

"Logical summing up? I would have thought that it showed you I was in no way responsible for my wife's death."

"Mm-m. Doctor, no matter what I might think, I really am not in a position to say to any person connected with any case—and that includes this one—that he or she is off the hook as far as I am concerned. What if I were to make a mistake, as I often do, and had to go to somebody who knew he was safe from arrest because I had said so, and put my hand on his shoulder? I have a revulsion for that happening. I have no qualms about going after a criminal who is on the *qui vive* because he knows I'm after him, but I hate potting at sitting ducks who are only sitting because I have tethered them by my own words of reassurance. So, doctor, even if you are as pure as driven snow, I shall not tell you so. I think you'll find that the innocent find their own consciences more of a reassurance than any words of mine."

"What I meant was that surely you now accept that there was no crime involved in my wife's death. Misadventure? An accident, perhaps, but no crime. Mrs Mace could not have done such a thing and I was not there."

"I see. But you know, doctor, even your colleague, Dr Spiller, feels guilt abut Mrs Bymeres' death."

"Why on earth should he?"

"Because when he prescribed M.A.O.I.s for your wife he

136

mentioned only cheese as a food to beware of."

"And he feels guilty because of that?"

"He's a conscientious doctor."

"Then he should know that every time a pharmacist makes up a prescription for M.A.O.I.s, he, the pharmacist, includes a leaflet giving all the foods to be avoided."

"I didn't know that."

"Why should you? But it stands to reason there must be that safeguard. M.A.O.I.s are given to neurotics. How many non-neurotics would be able to remember a long list of verbal instructions from a doctor, let alone patients with mental problems? No! The chemist hands out the list with the drug and if the patient then does something foolish like eating what is prohibited in black and white, then that's just too bad. This certainly isn't Spiller's fault."

"That's very magnanimous of you to say so."

"Oh, I know Spiller's a bit of an old fuss-pot and the sort to take a thing like this to heart, but I assure you there is no magnanimity on my part in exonerating him from all blame."

"Excellent," said Masters, getting to his feet. "Thank you for your time, doctor, and the coffee."

"Well, I can hardly say it's been a pleasure, but it has been an eye-opener to see how you work at close quarters."

Chapter 9

"D I D W E G E T him rattled, chief?" enquired Hill as they walked towards the car after leaving the surgery.

"A bit cross, perhaps. But he seemed pretty sure of himself. I can't decide whether that was vanity or a clear conscience. But whichever it was, he had something when he pointed out that he wasn't at the cottage for dinner and could prove that he didn't know the menu."

Hill unlocked the driver's door and leaned across to open the passenger door. There was silence until the car had been manoeuvred into the pre-lunch traffic stream and Masters had filled his pipe and got it going satisfactorily. Then Hill said: "I've got a feeling about him."

"Bymeres?"

"He's smug. I don't like smugness. It makes me think the worst of whoever is putting it across."

"That's a reason for being highly suspicious of him?"

"Perhaps not a reason. But it's a feeling I have. And feelings count for something."

"They do, indeed. Right fork ahead, I think. Yes, there's the sign. Step on it when you can."

Hill wondered why the unusual request for speed. Three reasons came to mind. Masters wanted to get back to Pilgrim's Cottage to see Mrs Mace, for non-investigatory reasons. Masters wanted to get back to Pilgrim's Cottage to hear what Green had learned. Masters had got hold of a little something which indicated that the case had begun to gel. Hill couldn't decide which of the three was the dominating reason for the hurry. Probably a combination of all of them, but when a case started to come sweet, Masters usually went broody. He had lapsed into thoughtful silence now, but Hill could not, for the life of him, see what in the recent interview could possibly have put a match to the final fuse that was going to crack the case. Not that that was particularly surprising. Masters had the habit of grabbing hold of apparent inessentials to use them, if not as the actual bricks of a case, at least as the mortar to keep the facts on course and help them stick together. It was a facility that Hill, and many others, envied. Some, chief among whom was Green, sneered at it, and regarded it as jam more than carefully mixed cement. But whatever it was, Hill hoped to be able to emulate Masters to some degree in the future. He was still speculating on what snippet in the recent interview could have been responsible for sparking off Masters' mind, when to his surprise, the superintendent spoke.

"Smug, you said?"

"That's right, chief."

"Define smug."

"Well, you know, smooth. Too twee in both his appearance and his manner."

"Not complacent and self-satisfied?"

Hill thought for a moment and then asked: "Was that your impression, chief?"

"I asked first."

"In that case, I reckon he was complacent in a way, but I'd say he was more self-satisfied than complacent."

"What's the difference?"

Hill was ready to explain. "Complacent? I reckon he was pleased with the way the interview went. But self-satisfied means I reckon he was pleased with himself and that's different from being pleased with, as it were, exterior things."

Masters leaned back. "I agree with you. I think he was self-satisfied. I don't believe we even dented his self-satisfaction, though we ruffled his complacency. He got angry with us, but not with himself."

"That's settled then. But where does it get us, chief?"

"Get us? Why, to the point of asking why he should be so all-fired self-satisfied. He's a vain man, true, but vanity such as his—based on professional ability, looks and so forth—is not the sort of trait which refuses to adapt to serious police questioning. We saw how Spiller reacted, and I'd say he was a vain man—as opposed to a self-satisfied one. So what is the usual cause of self-satisfaction?"

"Knowing you've got away with something, perhaps. Being a clever-dick who's managed to pull the wool over somebody's eyes."

"Something like that. But say, just for the sake of argument, that you have committed some crime which you know the police will lay at your door, but you have done it so cleverly that though they know you've done it, they can't bring it home to you. How self-satisfied would you feel then, as you see the cops floundering around trying to pin it on you and failing hopelessly?"

Hill thought for a moment before replying. Then he said: "We've often been in that boat, chief. We've known for certain who the villain was, but the case against him has fallen down through lack of evidence."

"That's virtually the story of our lives, I agree. But the people you're talking about haven't set out to commit a crime that they know we will pin on them. They've just hoped we would never get round to suspecting them. But if you embark on a crime where you can be certain the police *will* suspect you as the perpetrator, and then cover your tracks so cleverly that in spite of their certainty of your guilt, the police case must fail through lack of evidence, what then?"

"You get drunk on the thought of your own cleverness and become mightily self-satisfied—if you're fool enough to let yourself."

"As an inherently vain man will."

"Exactly, chief. So you've decided on Bymeres not because of what he said, or what he did or did not do, but because of his attitude."

"Shall we just say I think we should bear the possibility in mind, and concentrate on proving it."

"But if you intend to *concentrate* on proving it, it means you think Bymeres is Chummy, otherwise why concentrate?"

"Clever thinking," murmured Masters, and Hill suddenly realised that the chief had been using the journey to give him a lesson in thinking through a problem. Masters had not needed help. He had encouraged Hill to go through, step by step, this one facet of investigation which was above and beyond the scope of routine and written reports. It was a lesson intended to help him in the new job he would shortly be taking on, where he could no longer rely on Masters' mental ability or Green's phenomenal memory to pull the team through. Always before, Masters would merely have announced that he intended to concentrate on Bymeres, without explaining why. And when such decisions paid off, as they so often did, nobody bothered to wonder what the thought processes were behind such decisions. Now Hill realised that there was a logical progression from one stepping stone to another which any man could make, rather than a tremendous and successful leap in the dark which some saw as genius and regarded as luck or 'jam'.

"Thanks, chief."

"What for?"

"Going through it for me."

"If you've got enough nous to realise what I was up to, you'll do. Just remember that there are wheels within wheels and then go on to realise that those inside have to have a driving mechanism as well as those outside—even if it's only friction."

"I suppose that's how DI Green gets there—if he does."

"Yes. But he makes the mistake of always assuming that it is friction. So often it is an indirect drive, and you've got to ascertain from which direction it's coming."

A moment or two later they were passing through Long Munny and shortly turning into the gateway of Pilgrim's Cottage.

Hill was asked to fetch two more deck chairs from the garage.

"It's too late for coffee, I expect," said Wanda, "but there is beer in the refrigerator."

"Thank you."

Wanda smiled at him. "It will take me a few minutes to get it. You and Mr Green will want to talk, I expect. Would you like me to give a loud cough as I approach?"

"You must have had a reasonably pleasant interview," said Masters when Wanda had left them. "She seems happy enough."

"I'd say it's because she has a clear conscience," declared Green. "What I mean is, she's an intelligent woman who nevertheless makes what could be damning admissions without realising they are admissions because they are, to her, the truth. And I suppose the truth, in her view, hurts nobody."

"Has the interview been fruitful?"

"I'll say."

"And you pressed her on all the important points?"

"I did. But, as I said, being pressed for the truth isn't pressure to her. It's research in depth and as such is to be encouraged. She only got the willies once."

"When she heard that her food had caused her friend's death?"

"Say rather when she realised that nobody could have chosen a menu more calculated to be fatal."

"I get the point. But she appears to have recovered."

"Sure. You've come. And she's got a lot off her chest. That always has a lightening effect."

"Greeny, you're becoming quite the little trick cyclist. Anyhow, thanks for handling her so well; and now, before she gets back, tell me what you learned."

While Hill erected the two extra chairs, Green—aided by training and near-total recall—gave a full summary of the conversation between himself and Wanda. He had finished quite a few minutes before their hostess re-appeared.

"I took the opportunity to prepare my lunch," she explained. "I hope I didn't keep you waiting so long that your tongues are hanging out?"

"Mine," said Hill, rising to take over the chore of pouring the beer, "is cleaving. I don't know whether you've ever tasted the coffee in Dr Bymeres' surgery, but if you haven't, my advice is don't. Although, come to think of it, I don't think they'd dare serve it up like that, usually. I reckon we were treated to last week's dregs warmed up because the chief had a go at that old dragon, Miss Hector. She started coming the old acid with him, so he told her, and I suppose she thought she'd get her own back when Bymeres asked for coffee for us."

"Was it really as bad as that?"

"Mrs Mace, you've no idea. Still, never mind." He handed the glasses round. "Cheers!"

Masters drank and set his glass down.

"Mrs Mace, the DI has told me that your menu on Friday was an exact replica of that which Dr Bymeres ordered last Monday when he lunched with you."

"Not exactly exact. There was the game paté and the lemon mousse on Friday. David didn't have those on Monday."

"True. But you told the DI that Dr Bymeres pondered over his decision whether to choose pâté or liver."

"That is so."

"An attitude which, if deliberate, would be a good pointer to you as to what to include in a more comprehensive dinner menu."

"Both, you mean? I dare say you're right, if David could have known that his menu of Monday would be mine of Friday. And I swear he didn't."

"And yet—pursuing the hypothesis—had that been his objective, he could be said to have succeeded."

"Because I included the pâté, yes. But that doesn't mean that he gave the slightest hint or suggestion to me about Friday's bill of fare."

"You are positive of that?"

"Positive."

"I'll accept your word. But the other item missing from Monday's menu, the lemon mousse. You, yourself said that Dr Bymeres could have bet on that appearing at any dinner you gave at Pilgrim's Cottage, because it is the only pretty sweet you make well."

"That is true, too. But David didn't know I was inviting people in; that there was to be a dinner party."

"Does that matter? Whether there were to be three of you

or six, you would still have had to provide a meal, wouldn't you? I don't think you would have taken a chronic depressive out to dinner on her first night, would you?"

"Oh, no. Besides, David had to be here to get his nine-thirty bogus call."

"Quite."

"You've got it all wrong, you know. I decided on those dishes entirely alone."

"I'm sure. But why did you choose them?"

"Because I knew David would like them."

"A very reasonable and, I should think, a very usual thing to do for a woman who is providing an unaccustomed meal for the man she loves. Do you agree?"

"I suppose so."

"Now if I know that, don't you think Dr Bymeres does?"

"You mean he made sure last Monday that I knew which dishes would please him, in the knowledge that I would then provide them on Friday?"

"It bears thinking about. Did you know for instance that he liked clear soup?"

"Yes. He always has done."

"How would you normally clear soup, Mrs Mace?"

"With eggshells."

"I thought so. Yet the doctor did rather go on about how easy it is to make consommé with yeast extract, didn't he?"

"A bit."

"Liver and bacon. Had you ever known him choose that before? Or whole broad beans?"

"No. But I had known him eat pâté, often."

"Ah!"

"What have I said now?"

"If he has eaten pâté often, it would argue that he has a great liking for it. Yet on a hot day like last Monday, when you yourself ate cold food, he forgoes the pâté of which he is so fond in order to impress upon you his great liking for liver and whole beans, two foods you can never recall him eating before or, indeed, mentioning as favourites of his."

144

She looked at him miserably. "Do we have to go through the whole list?"

"Not just at the moment, if you'd rather we didn't. But I would like you to understand that I shall give similar consideration to every dish, and I can assure you that already there are arguments which can be brought to show why each of Dr Bymeres' choices last Monday was highly suspicious in our eyes."

"You sound as if you think he hypnotised me into choosing those foods."

"No, he didn't hypnotise you. Nothing quite so obvious. Besides, I would say you would be a difficult subject were you unwilling to be hypnotised, and I am extremely doubtful whether such a mild form of hypnosis as the doctor might practise at the luncheon table would last from Monday to Friday."

She bowed her head.

"Does the doc use hypnotic treatment?" asked Green. "I know a lot do."

"We didn't think of finding out," admitted Masters. "You see, we hadn't heard of last Monday's lunch when we were there, so there was no reason to ask."

Wanda, pale under the tan, looked up.

"He isn't a hypnotist. He doesn't believe in it."

"No?" He waited to see if she would continue. He was slightly surprised and just faintly dismayed when she said no more. Surprised because her statement had sounded to him like the beginnings of a longer explanation; and dismayed because she had defended Bymeres.

"You have obviously discussed the matter of hypnotism with him."

She nodded.

"At length?"

Again she nodded.

Masters tried a bow at a venture. "Was he, by any chance, a practising Suggestionist?"

She nodded a third time.

"A what?" asked Green.

145

"A Suggestionist. One who, on occasion treats disease by means of suggestion, when he finds a patient amenable to suggestion and when the disease to be treated is probably more imagined than suffered."

"I see."

"You think he suggestionised me?" asked Wanda.

"To some degree. There can be a great deal of power in suggestion."

"But I swear to you, it was just an ordinary lunch with ordinary conversation. I'm not his patient, remember."

"I remember. But nor are you just any old person outside his sphere of influence. When two people are as close as you two, the influence of each of you on the other is probably much greater than that of doctor on patient."

"You make it sound very beastly."

"I don't intend to. In fact, I'm sure I'd be right in saying the happier and better the relationship, the greater the mutual influence can be. Forgive this next question, please...." Masters paused and frowned, and Hill noticed that he was sweating as if in agony. "Would you mind telling me if there was any physical contact at the lunch table?"

"Physical...? I don't think I...."

"Did he lean across and hold your hand, for instance?"

"Yes. Yes he did." It was whispered unhappily.

Masters turned to Green and Hill. "You can probably guess that in such a relationship, the physical contact does impress or influence or at least reinforces verbal suggestion."

Green nodded. "That's plain enough. But nobody holds hands across a table at lunchtime except love-lorn teenagers."

"What you are saying," said Wanda quietly, "is that such a gesture is so unlikely in such a place at such a time that it was deliberate and calculated to influence me."

"To some degree," agreed Masters.

"I just don't believe it."

"I hope it isn't true."

"You're accusing David of murdering Daphne and of using me as his instrument."

Nobody replied.

146

"I see that is what you do think." It was a pitiable little answer to her own question. It seemed to Masters that she had suddenly realised that by using her in this way, Bymeres could not have held the slightest respect for her: could never have loved her. When a proud woman arrives at this conclusion there is no hiding the emotions. Wanda started to weep quietly.

Masters nodded to Green and Hill. The two withdrew down the garden. Masters had to go on one knee to put an arm round her shoulders. She yielded to the pressure of his arm, and he escorted her, head still bowed, into the cottage.

"You reckon we've cracked it?" asked Hill.

Green offered his, by now, crumpled Kensitas packet. "We've cracked it all right. He told me that the two of you came to the conclusion that Bymeres had engineered it before you ever heard of the grub."

"That's right. The chief said we'd have to concentrate on proving it."

"We can concentrate all right. But proof's going to be another thing. The clever bastard wasn't here at dinner, was he? And he didn't know what was for dinner either, did he? He can prove that—or rather, we can't prove that he did. And it's all right talking about this suggestivity malarky, but you bring that up in court and see where it gets you."

"So you reckon we're stuck."

Green sniffed reflectively.

"You do reckon so, don't you?"

"Look, laddie, what are we out to get? A case or justice?"

"Both."

"Right, Mr Smarty Pants, but not one at the expense of the other."

"No."

"Joe Egg says Bymeres is guilty. Right?"

"He's pretty sure."

"And we've got to prove means, motive and opportunity."

"Right."

"You do realise, don't you matey, that by tying in Mrs

Mace with Bymeres we could get them into the dock now, with every chance of a conviction?"

"You mean to send him down, we'd have to send her down, too?"

"Just that! Why should we take her word for it that he didn't know the menu any more than we should take his that he didn't know his wife was on these fancy drugs?"

"He still wasn't here at dinner."

"He didn't have to be, did he, if they were in cahoots?"

"I see."

"Means—the wrong food on top of drugs. Motive—the chance of getting rid of Mrs B. so that Mrs Mace can step into her shoes. Opportunity—Mrs B. being put on M.A.O.I.s. Bymeres would expect this at some time as he probably knew Spiller believed in drug holidays."

"You're forgetting something, aren't you?"

"You mean our friend there in the cottage will be fighting like hell to separate his lady-love from any implication in Bymeres' little plot?"

"Not that, although he'll obviously do his damndest for her. No, what I meant was that Mrs Bymeres ate the food although she'd been warned not to."

"I don't get it?"

"The chief probably hadn't time to tell you, but Bymeres told us that when he hands patients a load of M.A.O.I. drugs on prescription, the chemist always gives them a leaflet with a list of prohibited foods. So even if Spiller was a bit lax in only warning her off cheese, she'd have got the list in writing. So why did she eat what she shouldn't have done?"

Green wiggled a little finger in one ear, which was a fair indication that Hill had momentarily stumped him. Then he said: "It's going to be a bit of a dog's breakfast if this turns out to be suicide."

"Suicide by eating dinner? There's going to have to be a hell of a lot of coincidences accepted before anybody will agree to that."

"Maybe. But pretty strange things can happen. What if Mrs Bymeres thought her hubby was trying to get rid of her? She'd hate Mrs Mace because of it, her being the woman he wanted, so to speak. So she comes down here to see how the land lies. When she sees what's for dinner—all the wrong foods provided by the woman she hates she thinks here's her chance to get both of them. Instead of refusing the food she eats it, knowing it'll likely kill her and that hubby and his girl friend will be accused of murder and put away for life. That'd be a sweet revenge for a woman who knows she'll never be normal again. The thought of pretty Wanda growing old and haggard behind bars, and her smooth husband dressed for the rest of his life in prison denims might have driven her to it. What d'you think about that?"

"It's ingenious, I'll say that. But a bit far-fetched."

"But it wouldn't be if we decided to accept that Wanda didn't know anything about the prohibited foods, and that Dr Bymeres would have stopped his wife eating them had he not unfortunately been called away before dinner."

"What about the other loose ends? The duplication of the menu, for instance?"

"I'll admit that takes some swallowing," agreed Green. "Have you got a fag? I've been sharing mine all morning."

Masters eased her gently on to the settee and sat beside her. He offered her the white silk handkerchief he always carried in his breast pocket. She took it without a word. After a few moments she was sufficiently recovered to look up at him. He noticed that she had wept prettily. The tears had not made her eyes red-rimmed, smudged make-up, or disfigured her cheeks.

"What happens now?" she asked quietly, listlessly.

"As far as you're concerned? Nothing. Or at least not at the moment. You just rest here until I come or get in touch with you again."

"And David?"

"He's still got a few more questions to answer." He got to his feet. "There's one more I must ask you, too."

"What is it?"

"I don't want you to think this is in any way personal.

149

What I mean is, it is a genuine question asked in the course of police investigations. Did you love Dr Bymeres?"

"Love? The word love was never uttered by either of us at any time."

"That sounds to me as though he didn't love you or you him, yet you had a close relationship."

"A physical relationship. It seems to me now that we were both animals."

"Don't belittle yourself."

"Why not? I knew David never loved me, but I thought at one time I could grow to love him. Not that I ever did, but in spite of that I let him ... oh, hell! Has one got to be in love before one lets a man share one's bed? I thought that it would bring us closer, but we neither of us ever thought of marriage, so probably I was deluding myself and just indulging my farmyard appetite."

"Thank you for telling me. Now, either go and rest or get out in the garden and do some weeding. Anything to employ both mind and body. Understood?"

"If you say so. You are coming back?"

"This evening. Not before. I'm coming here to have supper with you. Would you like me to bring something in?"

She brightened up slightly. "If you're really coming, it will give me something to do—to prepare it, I mean. And you needn't bring anything."

"Right. And if David Bymeres calls, refuse to speak to him."

"I can't do that."

"Yes you can. Say you can't talk because the house is full of policemen."

She tried to smile. "All right."

The three of them met at the car.

"Got her calmed down?" asked Green.

"Enough to be going on with."

"What now, chief? Lunch?"

"I suppose so. Lord, it's after one o'clock. We'll have to make it a quickie. There's much to be done."

150

Hill started up and backed the car to face the gate. Green, in the back, asked: "Like what?"

"Like going over it all again."

"What?"

Masters half-turned in his seat to speak to them both. "I know Bymeres is guilty of murder. But I haven't got enough proof. I want to pin it on him. So we go over everything, looking for something we've missed. The alternative is to go to the Director of Public Prosecutions with yards of circumstantial evidence and ask him to decide whether we should charge Bymeres on what we've got. If he decides against, then Bymeres will go scot-free. The man who committed the perfect murder! I don't fancy letting him get away with it."

"Neither do I," agreed Green promptly, "but I'd like your assurance that we're not just going to flog a dead horse."

"How do you mean?"

"Don't get me wrong, but you did tell us yourself that you have a personal interest in Mrs Mace. Is this thrash going to be solely on her behalf?"

"I can't give you the assurance you ask," replied Masters quietly. "On two counts. First, because I have a personal interest in Mrs Mace, and it would be idle to pretend that clearing her doesn't interest me. Second, I genuinely believe she is innocent of any complicity in this case, and so—in order to see justice done, if nothing else—we must try to solve the problem. And that means involving Bymeres to a degree that will lead to his trial."

"Well at least you're being honest about it," grunted Green. "Have you got any ideas on how we're to go about it? I mean, you don't want us to conduct the same interviews over again, do you? Taking Mrs Mace through it all once more would drive her bonkers."

"I may have misled you. When I said go over it all again, I really meant looking for testing places. For instance the local people looked into that call Bymeres got before dinner. So far we've taken their word for it that it was true bill. We'll test it. You never know what we might learn. Then there's this business of Mrs Bymeres getting a cautionary leaflet

151

from the chemist. And another thing—did Mrs Bymeres have any money? We'd better check if that could be a motive for killing her. There are several other points we can test."

"Fair enough. But first, what about a dirty great pint from the wood? I'm clammed."

Chapter 10

HILL PULLED THE car up outside the white-painted semi-detached house shortly after half past two.

"I made the mistake of treading on her toes this morning," said Masters, "so be prepared for a frosty reception from our Miss Hector, particularly as she will be on her home ground and mistress of all she surveys."

"Would you like me to deal with her?" offered Green. "I've blunted a few old battleaxes before now. My skin's thicker than yours."

Masters stared at him in surprise. Green was still Green, but he was at least being abrasively co-operative on this case rather than abrasively unhelpful as in the past.

"Thanks. I'd better try to handle her if only for the sake of my own morale. But be prepared to chip in if I'm quelled with a look."

"Okay. Let's go."

Miss Hector answered the bell. She was in fawn slacks, cut very full to accommodate her comfortable sitting area. Her upperworks were covered by what looked like a hand-painted peasant blouse in cheese cloth. She wore gardening gloves and was carrying a pair of roll-cut secateurs.

"Forgive our calling on you at your home, Miss Hector, but we did call at the surgery, only to be told that you are off duty until half past four."

"Couldn't your business wait till then? I am trimming the dead heads in the garden."

"We *are* police, ma'am," Green reminded her gently. "And you look like the sort of person who would want to support the police."

Masters was almost expecting to hear him say 'and bring

153

back hanging and the cat', but Green had read the situation correctly. An appeal by the forces of law and order won the day. Miss Hector stood aside to let them enter the little hall and then ushered them into her sitting room. The uncut moquette three piece in grey-blue with a touch of pink in the pattern looked solid enough to take them. Miss Hector left her gloves in the hall, but came in still clutching the secateurs as though they would be some protection, however modest, against the worst that the three men—who must have topped forty-five stones between them—could do.

She took the chair nearest the empty fireplace, its sootiness suitably hidden by a fan of faded pink paper. Masters sat opposite while Green and Hill occupied the settee.

"Well," she asked impatiently, "what do you want?"

There seemed to be no point in beating about the bush. Masters came straight to the point. "We wish to ask you some questions about Dr Bymeres, Miss Hector."

The reply was prim, holier-than-thou. "He is one of my employers, you know."

"Nevertheless, my information is that you are not his greatest admirer, ma'am."

"What has that to do with Mrs Bymeres' death?"

"Your dislike of her husband? Quite a lot, I think. It could mean that because of your dislike or mistrust you will be more observant of his, shall we say, shortcomings, than others."

"And if I am?"

"Mrs Bymeres has been killed, Miss Hector. My job is to find out how, why and by whom. In any case such as this, the immediate members of the dead person's family must be investigated thoroughly."

"To incriminate them?"

"Or clear them."

"Have you investigated Mrs Mace thoroughly?"

"You know of Mrs Mace? The dead woman's friend?"

"Friend? I see you have not investigated her very thoroughly."

"Perhaps not thoroughly enough, but it may be that we

154

shall be able to repair that omission, as it is apparent that you know something about her that you think we ought to know."

"She is Dr Bymeres' mistress."

"Is that common knowledge at the surgery?"

"Nobody knows but me." The voice was triumphant.

"That is interesting. You have proof of it, Miss Hector?"

"The proof of my own eyes. Last autumn I still had a week's leave owing to me. Because it was too late to go far afield, I decided to have a short break at the Four-Fingered Hand in Long Munny."

"Close to Pilgrim's Cottage, where Mrs Mace lives?"

"And Mrs Bymeres died."

"I take it that during your stay there you saw something of which you didn't approve."

"Didn't approve? I should just think I did. Mrs Bymeres was a cousin of our senior partner...."

"Was she, now? I didn't know that."

"Well, second cousin, really. A dear girl, full of life and fun until her husband finally drove her into a mental breakdown. And he owed what he had to her, you know. He was only taken on by the partnership because of his wife."

"His ability as a doctor wasn't taken into account?"

"Oh, he was clever enough, I dare say. But he got the job through her."

"I see. You were going to tell us what happened on your holiday in Munny."

"On my first evening there I was returning from a walk when I saw Dr Bymeres' car parked outside the hotel. I recognised it, naturally—the yellow Renault 17—apart from knowing the number. Of course, I hadn't told anybody I was going to Long Munny. I prefer to keep my business private. But I felt it would be pleasant to meet somebody I knew there, and I thought perhaps Mrs Bymeres might be with her husband. So I looked into the bars in the hope of locating them. I found the doctor, but he didn't see me. I withdrew as soon as I saw he was escorting a blonde. They were sitting drinking at the bar and obviously very friendly."

"And you knew his companion was Mrs Mace?"

"Not then. But I saw his car three times that week, parked outside a delightful cottage in Little Munny. Always at times when I would have thought he would have been on his rounds or at home with his wife. I considered it my duty to ask to whom the cottage belonged. I was told the owner was Mrs Mace, a divorcee."

"And you told nobody of this?"

"Nobody. I am in a position of trust and I know how to hold my tongue."

"Of course. Did you know, too, that Mrs Mace was also a great friend of Mrs Bymeres?"

Miss Hector sniffed. "There are friends and friends."

"True. But that is why she visited the cottage for a holiday."

"She was obviously unaware of her husband's carryings-on."

"Almost certainly. But I understand that Dr Bymeres' visits to Mrs Mace have not been so frequent lately. It is said that pressure of work leaves him less time now than at one time."

"That is absolute nonsense."

"Is it? I was told that with other doctors going off on holidays from Easter onwards, Dr Bymeres' workload would be heavier."

"Lighter, if anything."

"Perhaps you would explain?"

"In the practice, Superintendent, there are eight doctors, each of whom has six weeks' holiday a year. As no more than one is allowed to be away at the same time, you can see that except for the four weeks of January, which is our busiest month for colds and flu, we never have more than seven doctors on call, but we never have less than seven. So absence does not cause the workload to fluctuate to any great degree."

"I see. I didn't know that."

"Neither, apparently, did you know that at this time of the year—high summer—the individual workload for each doctor decreases appreciably. From the beginning of spring, through

156

to autumn, colds, flu, chilblains, bronchitis and all the other ailments closely associated with winter weather lessen in number. The result is, if anything, that Dr Bymeres has had more time at his disposal for philandering."

"I am exceedingly grateful for so clear an explanation, Miss Hector. Now, with your permission, I would like to turn to last Friday evening."

"What about it?"

"Dr Bymeres has told me that you agreed to ring him at half past nine to give him an excuse to leave Pilgrim's Cottage. Is that true."

"Perfectly true."

"Why did you agree to such a deception?"

"He told me that if he didn't get a call he would be obliged to spend the weekend at the cottage. I was loth to agree to the bogus call, but I realised that at least it would mean he would be away from his mistress. Also, had he stayed, I felt that his relationship with Mrs Mace might become apparent to Mrs Bymeres, and I would agree to anything to prevent her being hurt."

Masters nodded understandingly. "But in the event, that bogus call was unnecessary."

"It was. As I was about to leave the surgery, a Mrs Cupwell rang. She told me that Dr Bymeres had instructed her to ring for him at any time should her husband have severe pain. Her story was correct because she said Dr Bymeres had told her he was going to Little Munny for the evening and, if called, was prepared to return to attend Mr Cupwell."

"Can you tell me what Mr Cupwell is suffering from—without breaking any ethical code, of course?"

"If I don't tell you, I suppose you will visit the poor man?"

"Our job often has unpleasant facets, Miss Hector."

"He has terminal cancer."

"Has he! And you said 'severe pain'?"

"I did."

"Correct me if I'm wrong, but I thought all terminal
157

patients at the stage where severe pain might supervene, would be kept under heavy sedation."

"That is my belief, too."

"Then why not Mr Cupwell?"

"I really have no idea. All I can tell you is that Dr Bymeres visited the patient at about two o'clock last Friday afternoon. He worked through the lunch hour—or so he said —because he wanted to be free, later in the afternoon to drive his wife to Little Munny."

"He visited at two o'clock? Would he have administered an analgesic at that time?"

"According to the patient record, the doctor believed it was time for Mr Cupwell to change from oral analgesics to injected ones. The first injection was administered that day."

"And by early evening the effect had worn off and Mrs Cupwell, following the doctor's instructions, phoned to say her husband was uncomfortable."

"That is correct. It was a genuine call."

"Thank you, Miss Hector. There are just two more things you can probably help us with. First, do you happen to know who Mrs Bymeres' solicitor is?"

"That is very easy. She uses the practice solicitor. Mowbray and Tulley on Pike Road. Not a quarter of a mile from the surgery."

"Thank you. And the second question is: which pharmacy usually made up her prescriptions?"

"That I cannot be sure about. But I would think she went to Mr Blundell, an excellent man, whose premises are close to her home on Victoria Road."

"Wonderful. You have been a great help to us, Miss Hector. These cases are always distressing to close friends of the deceased, but we must try our level best to find out the cause of the tragedy."

Miss Hector rose to her feet, still clutching her secateurs. "I can make no guess as to the cause, but you would do well to look closely at Mrs Mace. Any woman who would steal a sick friend's husband must be suspect."

"I shall bear your words in mind, ma'am."

"Cor," said Green. "I never got a word in. She's got the gift of the gab, that old faggot."

"But profitable, wouldn't you say?"

"How come? All we learned was that Bymeres had apparently gone off Mrs Mace a bit of late, and that the call that brought him back home was genuine."

Masters got into the car beside Hill. "Try the solicitor's office first."

"Wait a moment," said Green. "You reckon the old bag told us something more, don't you?"

Hill drew away.

"We'll need to check with somebody like Theddlethorpe, but as I understand it, most analgesic injections last effectively for an average of about four hours. They may vary a bit each way, and you've got to add on twenty minutes or so before they start to work, and probably another twenty at the other end for them to peter out completely."

"That makes about four and three quarter hours all told."

"The injection was given at two o'clock."

"So Cupwell would be in pain by a quarter to seven. It adds up. By the time his missus got through to the surgery and the Hector bird got in touch with Bymeres it would be seven o'clock."

"I've got it!" said Hill.

"Fine. Tell the DI," invited Masters.

"If we know how long the effect of a jab lasts, so does Bymeres. He knew Cupwell would need attention before seven o'clock, so he gives Mrs Cupwell his address in the country and assures her he will return if her husband is in pain."

"What about that?" Masters asked Green.

"You mean he fixed that call? He knew all along it would come?"

"Right. The one at nine-thirty was to fool us—and other people. The one at seven was to get him away from Pilgrim's Cottage before dinner."

"That nobbles the bastard!"

"Not quite. But I think it proves to our satisfaction that he planned it and planned it alone. Anybody disagree?"

Hill pulled into the kerb. "Mowbray and Tulley, chief. Commissioners for Oaths among other things."

"Good. All we want to know is if Mrs Bymeres had any property to leave."

"In her own name," said Masters, "less than a couple of thousand. The house is in both names, and it's worth quite a lot, but that's immaterial."

"Chicken feed," agreed Green. "So she wasn't bumped off for her money. No doctor in a good practice is going to murder his wife for a couple of thousand."

"Where now, chief? The chemist's?"

"Please."

Green selected a bent Kensitas. "So why did he kill her? It wasn't because of Mrs Mace. He'd been seeing less and less of her, when he could have seen more and more, and she says that neither of them ever thought about marriage."

"You tell me," invited Masters.

"Okay, so you reckon you know."

"I'll make a guess and back it up with a reason or two."

"Let's hear it."

"He has another woman in tow, whom he *does* wish to marry."

Green stared at him, the cigarette dangling from his lower lip. "Yeah?"

"Here's my deduction. Although he has more time at his disposal, he visits Mrs Mace less frequently. Why?"

"He wants to spend his time with the other bird."

"Why not? I don't suppose he spent it with his wife."

"I'll bet he didn't."

"He wants to marry her. To divorce his wife would take at least three years, and that's a long time if some luscious piece is getting a bit demanding."

"He could give his wife grounds, in order to speed it up a bit."

160

"He could. But he's a doctor and a vain man. Would he want to be in the wrong? And it would still take years."

"Okay. I'll go along with that."

"Now let's examine his modus operandi. Think of the phone calls. One out in the open, the other a secret. Why not the same with his women? Mrs Mace? He doesn't shout about her from the rooftops, but he doesn't go out of his way to hush it up unduly. The Mystery Woman? He keeps her so well out of sight that even Miss Hector doesn't suspect her presence, otherwise she'd have said so—to us at least."

"She'd have known," agreed Green. "And you reckon that the miserable bastard used a fine woman like Mrs Mace to murder his wife at second-hand?"

"I believe so. It fits, you know."

Green nodded. "So now what have we got to do? Find this other woman?"

"The woman," said Hill, "he was so keen to come home for last Friday night. No wonder he didn't go back."

"Hold it," said Green. "He was at home when Mrs Mace rang him last Saturday morning."

"He would be, wouldn't he? He was expecting the call."

Again Green nodded.

There was silence until Green halted outside Mr Blundell's pharmacy.

The shop was one of the old family chemists. Scrupulously clean, it owed nothing to chromium, plastic and powder colours. Mahogany, thick bevelled glass in heavy display cupboards, gold-leaf transfers on drawers, a small gas jet flaring gently to melt the wax for sealing wrapping paper, and on the topmost shelf, under an ornate ceiling, widely spaced gallipots that, Masters guessed, many a collector would give his ears for. The cobalt blue putti and motifs stood out bright against the crazed yellowing glaze of each hand-thrown jar. It was like a whiff of yesterday to Masters, reminiscent of childhood days when chemists were chemists and not supermarkets.

"Mr Blundell?"

The man behind the counter was bespectacled. He would

161

be about sixty, but some trick of nature, or a shock, had left him with one side of his still-full head of hair snow white, while the other side was just greying from its earlier blackness. His military-style white coat, collared round the throat, gave an impression of clinical preparedness.

"Yes, sir. What can I do for you?"

The two women assistants were busy at the other counter. Masters could talk freely.

"I am Superintendent Masters of Scotland Yard, Mr Blundell. At the moment I am enquiring into the sudden death of a woman who may have been a customer of yours."

"Are you referring to Mrs Bymeres, the doctor's wife?"

"So she did come to you to have her prescriptions made up."

"Always. The last time was a week last Saturday afternoon."

"You can remember exactly when each patient visited you?"

"Mrs Bymeres, certainly. She is a doctor's wife, and in my profession, Superintendent, the patronage of doctors and their families must be something of a cachet. At least I am old-fashioned enough to believe so. And, of course, Mrs Bymeres was something of a social acquaintance."

"Because of contacts due to business?"

"Oh, entirely. We met at functions rather than in a domestic setting."

"I see. Can you remember what Mrs Bymeres' last prescription was for?"

"May I know the reason why I should give you such confidential information?"

"Of course. Mrs Bymeres ate some food which reacted against her medicine. It killed her."

Blundell made no direct reply. Instead, he asked Masters to step round the counter and into the dispensary.

"Superintendent, one of the reasons why I remember so clearly that Mrs Bymeres came here a week last Saturday afternoon was because of something out of the ordinary that happened on that occasion."

"If it is pertinent to my enquiry, I should like to hear about it."

"I feel it could be pertinent in view of the fact that the prescription on that particular day was different from those usually presented by Mrs Bymeres. It was for M.A.O. inhibitors which, as you may or may not know, can be dangerous with certain nitrogenous foodstuffs, notably cheese."

"I am aware of the danger, Mr Blundell. What happened on that day?"

"Because of the danger of eating these prohibited foods when patients are on M.A.O.I.s, the drug manufacturers produce leaflets listing the foods. We include one of these leaflets with every prescription for M.A.O.I.s. But, as you may know, we dispense from very large packs. And sometimes—particularly if doctors have written prescriptions for small numbers of pills or capsules—the supply of leaflets may run out before the drugs themselves."

"Are you telling me that you gave Mrs Bymeres her prescription without the leaflet?"

"Please hear me out. I had the necessary drugs, but no leaflets. Remember it was late on Saturday afternoon. I felt I couldn't let Mrs Bymeres have her medicine without the leaflet, neither could I expect her to pass the weekend without her medicine. As I am under no legal obligation to supply the leaflet—although I accept the moral obligation unquestioningly—while Mrs Bymeres was waiting, I rang a fellow pharmacist and asked him if he could spare me a leaflet. He assured me that he could, so I immediately sent my girl to collect it."

"A standard of service one rarely receives these days," murmured Masters.

"Thank you."

"Did Mrs Bymeres wait?"

"No. I counted out her prescription and took it to her. I explained that certain foods were dangerous and she told me that her doctor had given her the same information. She actually mentioned cheese...."

"Anything else?"

"You mean did she list the foods? No. But I took it for granted that Dr Spiller had warned her suitably, and in any case, as I told her, she would be getting a full list. I told her I would deliver it to her house myself about an hour later, on my way home."

"And did you?"

"Of course. The girl brought three or four leaflets back. I put one of them into an envelope, put Mrs Bymeres' name on it and my rubber stamp, and dropped it into Dr Bymeres' letter box as I went past immediately after shutting the shop. And that is why I remember Mrs Bymeres' last visit so vividly."

"Thank you. You have helped me a great deal."

"Are you at liberty to . . . ?"

"She was away for the weekend. On an evening when her husband was not present, her hostess—unaware of the danger to her guest—served up some of the prohibited foods. Mrs Bymeres ate them."

"But if she had read the leaflet . . ."

"Quite, Mr Blundell. Or if only her husband had been present to stop her. But far from any blame attaching to you, I can assure you that my personal view is that your action in sending for the leaflet and delivering it yourself must have emphasised to Mrs Bymeres, as the mere inclusion of the leaflet certainly would not have done, the importance of avoiding the prohibited foods."

"Poor woman! Probably her mind was wandering a little. Acute depression, you know, can play all sorts of tricks with the memory and a person's awareness generally."

"So I am led to believe. It doesn't make my task any easier, but your explanation has really helped me. Thank you, Mr Blundell."

Masters shook hands, bade the chemist good afternoon and rejoined his colleagues in the car.

"Corn in Egypt?" enquired Green.

Masters settled in his seat. "Perhaps not bushels of it, but probably a few gleanings." He recounted the interview with Blundell while they remained parked at the pavement.

"Now where do we go for honey?"

"We have to try and trace that leaflet."

"Did the locals find it at Mrs Mace's pad?"

Masters didn't answer, but looked at Hill, who took out his notebook from which he retrieved a folded sheet of paper with a typewritten list.

"It's not mentioned, chief. But it could be included as part of the drugs found, without being listed separately."

"I think not. I don't think they would be so lax as to lump it together with the drugs without reading it to see that it was connected with them, and if they'd read it they'd have known what killed her without calling on a pathologist."

"Sounds sense," grunted Green. "So where is it? At her house, or destroyed?"

"Let's talk it through," suggested Masters, "because I'm strongly of the opinion that she didn't read it, otherwise she wouldn't have eaten that dinner. I mean, even allowing for some loss of memory due to her condition, an item as rare as beans in their pods would strike some chord. And from what we've gathered so far, I think she was not all that bad—not a real nut case, I mean. Just excessively withdrawn and disturbed."

"I'll buy that," said Green. "So if she didn't read it, did she ever get it?"

Hill slapped the back of his seat. "I've got it, chief. It was that leaflet that gave Bymeres the idea for murdering her."

Green glanced at Masters and then back to Hill. "You know, laddo, just every so often you produce a rabbit. You might make a go of it in your new job after all."

"You think I'm right?"

"Of course you are," said Masters. "This is how I see it. Blundell puts the leaflet in an envelope, franks it with his own rubber stamp and writes Mrs Bymeres' name on it. He pushes it into the house letter box. Now, who would be accustomed to picking up the mail in that household?"

"The doc himself. They get scads of letters—mailed and brought by hand."

"Right. So Bymeres takes the envelope, whether it was alone or not. It has the name Bymeres on it and a pharmacist's stamp. Who's it for? Ninety-nine chances out of a hundred it's for the doc himself, because apart from getting nearly all the mail, Blundell's stamp shrieks out that its contents are of a medical nature. So, Bymeres opens it—and it doesn't matter whether he did it deliberately or by mistake, though I think the latter is more likely. As soon as he sees the list he realises what has happened. His wife has been put on to M.A.O.I.s, but so far it looks as though she hasn't been properly briefed about the prohibited foods."

"Just a moment, chief! How would he know a conscientious doctor like Spiller hadn't told her?"

"Don't muck it up, son," counselled Green. "Bymeres could soon find out. All he's got to do is suggest to his missus that they have Welsh Rabbit for supper. She says no because Spiller has said no cheese. Has he? What else has Spiller said you haven't to have? Nothing, but there is a list. Mr Blundell was going to bring one. Was he? Well, there isn't one in the letter box. Never mind, I can tell you. Don't eat oysters, caviar, or chilli con carne and lay off the vodka and ouzo. Everything else is okay."

"You reckon that's how it was, chief?"

"Could be. But even if some such graphic interview between husband and wife did not take place, I don't think Bymeres would have minded too much."

"How d'you mean?"

"If she didn't know what to avoid—as opposed to his planting false information in her mind—she'd eat Mrs Mace's dinner. If she did know what to avoid—say by consulting one of her husband's books perhaps, because it's clear she didn't ask Blundell or Spiller—then all that would have happened is that he would have failed for the time being. I think it was a chance he could afford to take, because if it didn't come off, nobody would ever have regarded it as an attempt on Mrs Bymeres' life. He would be free to try again in some

166

other way. But when I said I don't think he would have minded too much, I'm not suggesting he'd not have been annoyed at failure. He would, but it would not have cost him dear. He's a vain man and failure would be a blow to his vanity."

"If you're right, chief, and he's got another bird tucked away whom he wants to be free to marry eck dum, he wouldn't have liked failing."

"There's that, of course."

Green offered Hill a crumpled Kensitas. "What are we going to do?"

"I'd like to find that list."

"If he found it, wouldn't he have chucked it away?"

"I think not. You see, Blundell can say he took it there. It's unlikely that Mrs Mace would have destroyed her own medical instructions. That's the sort of thing I imagine any patient would be careful not to do. So if it were missing, somebody might begin to wonder who had disposed of it."

"And as it wasn't with her at the cottage, it should be in the house."

"Right."

"We need a warrant."

"I'd like to have a look without Bymeres knowing."

"Any particular reason? I mean we've got him, haven't we?"

"Even so, I'd like to break him down, just in case what we've got is not enough. And he's only going to be broken down if we can present him with a sudden shock. I want that list and something to show me who the other woman is."

"Chief," said Hill, "it's Monday afternoon. I don't know whether Bymeres is at home or not. But if you and the DI were to go and ring his front door bell while I sort of sauntered round the back...."

Masters and Green exchanged glances.

"Understand, Sergeant, that in no circumstances, no circumstances at all, must you remove anything from the house. If we are accused of unlawful breaking, I'm prepared to plead that we called in the normal course of duty and found signs of entry, and I reckon we'd get away with it as long as we hadn't lifted anything."

"Right, chief. Nothing to be touched. There's a pair of gloves in the compartment...."

It was a pleasant, tree-lined road, with little patches of well-kept grass dividing pavement from roadway. The car went unnoticed among the half dozen or so already parked outside houses. Nobody was about. The sleep of the afternoon hung over everything. A distant mower did just break the silence, but even its regular rhythm was soporific rather than alerting.

When Masters and Green returned to the car after fruitlessly ringing the front door bell, Masters said: "While remaining as inconspicuous as possible, keep your eyes skinned to the back in case he comes. I'll watch the front. It will be easy enough to head him off to allow Hill time to get clear."

Green grunted and slid down in his seat. "I'll just gizz through the driving mirror. Yellow Renault 17, isn't it?"

"That's it." Masters packed his pipe and lit up. The two smoked in silence for the best part of ten minutes.

"The sergeant's a useful hand," said Green eventually.

"Meaning that he's going to be a great loss to us?"

"Us?"

"That's what I said. That's what I meant."

"Why?"

"We've lost Brant. Hill's going. If you were to go as well, I'd need a complete new team." Masters turned. "I'll be honest with you, Willy P. If I could have stopped Brant—without disrupting his prospects and his marriage—I would have done. If I could have kept Hill without stopping his promotion, I'd have done that, too. Your move I can stop. It's up to you, because we've both tried to get rid of each other in the past. But forgetting that, if you say the word, I'll fix it for you to stay."

"You're not begging me to?"

"No. Simply offering you the option. Hell, man, we haven't got on, but even so, I, for one, am not prepared to see a man with as much to offer as you have, hawking his services round the Divisions. So you're not the world's best ambassador. But you don't have to be. You're a copper."

"Thanks."

"Does that mean you want to stay?"

"I'm enjoying this case."

"Typical. Start to enjoy yourself on what could have been your last outing with the firm."

Green sat up. "He's been a long time gone, hasn't he?"

"A quarter of an hour? Give him another five, seeing it's so quiet."

"Two of us would have got through quicker."

"Maybe. But you haven't got gloves."

Green settled down again. Masters was aware that though the DI was making no sound, his body was almost purring with satisfaction. Masters, himself, was aware of a slight sense of irritation, not at having offered to keep Green, but at the circumstances which had made the offer inevitable. He glanced at his watch again. Hill must have been unlucky, or he'd have been out by now.

They had to wait another seven minutes before Hill came through the gate. His gloves were off and in his jacket pocket. As he climbed into the car, he said: "A window slightly open, chief, and the back door on a Yale. All left tickety-boo."

"Come on," said Green. "You're bottling something back."

"The list is there, in the top drawer of her bedside table. Right on top of various bottles and packets of plasters. She obviously uses it as her private medicine chest."

"You didn't touch anything?"

"Never laid a finger, chief. I got the impression it had been planted pretty carefully. There was one of those emery board nail files laid exactly along a line on the paper, with its end level with the last letter of some print. But I could read it nearly all."

"Good. We'll have to find it officially, of course."

"Of course."

"So what kept you?" asked Green.

"The phone list."

"How come?"

"It's one of those alphabetical push-button jobs. I thought I ought to have a glance at it."

"And?"

"Under 'I' stroke 'J' there was a number which wasn't opposite a name. Everything else seemed all above board. Doctor and Mrs This, Mary Smith, John Jones—you know the sort of thing. I reckoned if he didn't want his missus to know he might just pencil in the number of his girl-friend under her initial. Other than that there was nothing I could see."

"You got the number, I hope," said Green.

Hill opened his notebook and held it up for Green to see.

"Okay, matey, I'll get on to the Yard and ask them to trace it. Stop at the first box."

Hill started the car up.

"While you're at it," said Masters, "ring the local nick and say we want a warrant for the Bymeres house. Don't make a song and dance. Just suggest that it seems to be the thing to do to have a look at the dead woman's belongings. Say we're on our way there to collect it now."

Chapter 11

THEY FOUND THE local police station and called on DI Wrotham in his office.

"How're you getting on, sir?"

Masters took a seat and stretched his legs. "We're hopeful."

"What of?"

"Delivering it to you all signed and sealed."

"May I know who ... ?"

"Not yet," grunted Green. "Sorry, chum, but this is a case where everything must be proved beyond doubt."

"But you're here. Haven't you come to tell me all about it?"

"Only to collect the search warrant for Bymeres' house and to wait for a call from the Yard."

"Oh! Well, the warrant is ready. I'll get it for you."

"Tell your lads to put any call for me through to here."

"Right." Wrotham left them.

"Now if that had been me," Green said, referring to the departing DI, "I'd have demanded to know what's going on. No wonder these characters have to call us in. They haven't enough interest in the job to cop anything except a school kid pinching toffee-apples."

"That's not it," said Hill. "We—that is the chief's firm—have a rep for pulling irons out of local fires. And reps are frightening things. If I didn't work with the chief I'd be scared to demand information from him myself. And don't forget you're part of the firm."

"Meaning?"

"Meaning we know you, but your manner with strangers isn't always as friendly as it might be. And they don't always realise that it's a front to hide your nervousness."

"My what?"

"Nervousness. Shyness. Something like that. You're tough on the outside and as soft as Joe Soap inside."

"Hell's bloody bells! The prospect of a bit of promotion is opening you up."

"What would it do for you?" Masters asked Green.

"Me? Why, I dunno. An' I'm never likely to find out again in my career, am I?"

The phone rang before Masters could reply. Green took the call, scribbling on Wrotham's blotter as he took down the message.

"Ingrid Jannery? J—A—double N—, yes, I've got it. Flat three, eleven Quorum Road ... yes, thanks. *Miss* Jannery. Okay. Ta!"

He put the phone down.

"Miss Ingrid Jannery."

"So she was under 'I' stroke 'J' in his book on either initial. Ask where Quorum Road is, please Hill."

As Hill went out, Wrotham came in with the folded warrant. "Your call came through?"

"Yes, thank you. We'll be on our way. Will you be here tomorrow morning?"

"What time?"

"Can we say ten o'clock. I hope to tell you all about it then."

"I'm anxious to know. So are the brass-hats. They've asked me two or three times already today."

Masters grinned. "They're always like that. Tell them to wait until tomorrow."

They collected Hill, who was studying the desk sergeant's street map.

"About two and a half miles, chief."

"What's the time?"

"Half past four, just gone."

"I wonder if she's a working girl?"

"Bound to be," said Green. "The flat's hers, seeing the phone's in her name. And misses living in their own flats in this day and age have to go out to earn the money to pay for

172

them. Like as not she works in the smoke and won't be home until six or seven."

"That sounds reasonable," agreed Masters.

"What about Bymeres?"

"Miss Hector said she had to be back on duty at half past four. That's likely to be half an hour before surgery starts. But Bymeres wouldn't arrive before five. Doctors don't often get there before time. So if he decided to have a cup of tea beforehand, we might catch him at home now. Anyway, we'll try."

Masters' assessment of the situation was correct. The yellow Renault was outside the house, and Bymeres answered the bell. He was in his shirt sleeves, and carrying a napkin.

"Good afternoon, doctor. I have a warrant to search the house. I'd like to do that now."

Bymeres did not appear to be surprised or in the least put out, though he did protest that he had a surgery in a quarter of an hour and it was time he was leaving. "I'm just finishing a cup of tea. There's still some cake left if you would like some."

"No, thank you, doctor. May we come in?"

"Of course." Bymeres stood back. "But at least tell me what you are looking for or expect to find, then I might be able to help you and I could get along to the surgery."

"That's very kind of you, doctor. I'm sorry about the surgery, but we did call earlier and you weren't in."

"I was visiting a patient in hospital. Now, what is it you want? Daphne died twelve miles from here. There cannot possibly be anything in this house to help you in your investigation."

Bymeres led the way into the sitting room where his tea tray was sitting on a low table.

"As a matter of fact," said Masters, "you put us on to this, doctor. Do you remember telling me this morning that pharmacists give an instruction leaflet when they dispense M.A.O.I.s?"

"I remember."

"It appears that when Mr Blundell gave Mrs Bymeres her

173

medicine a week last Saturday, he had run out of leaflets."

"Oh! So that's it. That's why she didn't know about the prohibited foods."

"Not quite, doctor. Mr Blundell delivered the leaflet himself that same evening. At about half past five."

"Really? I didn't see him. But I don't suppose I was at home at the time. Daphne would answer the door."

"The envelope was put into the letter box."

"I see. So she did get the warning after all."

"Apparently, she did, doctor. But you must see that it is important for us to establish that she did."

"Oh, why?"

"For a number of reasons. I mean it may be that Mrs Bymeres, having seen the list, might have decided that to eat prohibited foods while taking M.A.O.I.s might be an easy way of committing suicide. You never know."

Bymeres shook his head. "Not Daphne. I'll bet Spiller will tell you that in spite of her depression she was not suicidal. That would be one of the first things he'd establish in order to guard against it."

"So in spite of Blundell delivering it, you think she didn't get the leaflet?"

"I think she didn't read it—a slightly different matter."

"Of course. But if we were to find it, it might end speculation. Perhaps we should start in Mrs Bymeres' bedroom."

The doctor led the way upstairs. There were several drawers to examine in tallboy, chest and dressing table before Hill moved to the bedside close to where Bymeres was standing. Masters watched the doctor as Hill pulled the shallow drawer open.

"I think this must be it, chief." Hill did not touch the leaflet, and tried to sound as though the discovery was a happy surprise to him.

This was Bymeres' chance. "Where? Here, let me see, I'll tell you." He had picked up the black-printed stuffer before Masters made any attempt to stop him.

"I wish you hadn't done that, doctor."

"Why not? This is it. This is what you're looking for. She

174

did get it after all." He held the paper out to Masters who made no move to take it.

"Did she, Dr Bymeres?"

"What do you mean?"

"I mean that our fingerprint specialists are clever enough to tell us whether she ever handled it or not."

"What's up, doc?" asked Green, considerately. "You're looking a little pale."

"And," continued Masters, "if your wife's prints are not there, doctor, we shall want to know how the leaflet managed to get from the front door to Mrs Bymeres' drawer, and how it got out of Mr Blundell's envelope."

Bymeres stared at him, and then deliberately crumpled the leaflet into a ball.

"Steady on," said Green. "No need to get upset, doctor. It'll take a little longer, but it can still be smoothed out for testing. We can even trace the sweat from the fingers these days."

"How very clever of you."

"We have been very clever," admitted Masters. "At any rate clever enough to anticipate what you would do. You see, doctor, we guessed that you would not be wearing gloves when you opened your mail a week last Saturday and that you therefore probably touched the leaflet before you realised what it was. So it would have your prints on it, no matter how carefully you hid it before your wife's death and before placing it in her drawer after her death. That meant you had to make sure you handled it after it was found and in front of us, so that there was a ready excuse for your prints being on it. We knew what you would do. We let you do it. It confirmed what we already knew. That leaflet is, intrinsically, relatively unimportant.

"You were skilful, Bymeres. But not skilful enough. I should like you now to accompany us to the local police station where I shall in due course arrange for you to be charged with the murder of your wife.

"You will appreciate that your absence from Pilgrim's Cottage during dinner on Friday night will be no defence.

"Sergeant Hill will go with you to collect your jacket and accompany you to the car."

"And you can drop the leaflet in here, mate," said Green, holding out an opened plastic bag. "We might as well have it, just for laughs."

Wrotham accepted the prisoner quite calmly. "It had to be him, didn't it? I mean, I guessed."

"But proving it?"

"That would have been a bit more difficult, I suppose."

"Of course. I'll leave it to you to charge him. We have another call to make."

"She should be in now," said Green as they got into the car. "Nearly twenty to seven."

Hill started up. "I wonder what she's like, this Ingrid dame?"

"She'll be a smasher," said Green. "She may be a scrubber, too, but she'll be a smasher. She's got to be, hasn't she? Bymeres fancies himself, you know, so he's not going to want anything to do with a bird who's much less than perfect on the eye. Specially not when he'd got a looker like Mrs Mace already. This new one's got to have something Mrs M hasn't got."

"And," added Masters quietly, "she's got to be worth committing murder for, and worth jeopardising Mrs Mace's freedom for."

"Forgotten that," admitted Green. "But what you've got to remember, George, is that a chap like Bymeres could be dazzled by highly polished brass even when there's solid gold to be had for the asking."

"Thanks, Greeny. I know what you mean."

No more was said in the few minutes it took Hill to reach Quorum Road. It was a short street of Victorian villas, all built in much the same way with a semi-basement and three floors above. Masters guessed they were landlords' properties and were not owned by the occupiers. Some effort had been made to smarten them up and repair the ravages of time. But the once-gracious houses were now painted like raddled hags. Too much colour splashed on in the wrong places to hide the wrinkles. Front walls were bulging, stonework needed cleaning, and it seemed that none of the tenants wanted to know about the gardens.

It was difficult to find a parking spot at the kerb. Hill finally decided to run into a wide space which had been levelled between two of the houses, the back gardens of which had been largely given over to a row of lock-up garages. He pulled in. "If anybody wants to complain," he said, "let 'em."

No. 11 had a flight of outside steps. The large front door stood open. The bell-push captions said that Miss I. Jannery and flat 3 could be found on the first floor. Masters led the way up. The flat had been cut off from the stairway by the simple expedient of putting a door across the landing. Masters rang the bell.

The door opened after a moment or two.

"Hello, you're early toni——"

"Miss Jannery?" Masters recognised the face. He had seen it in cosmetic advertisements on TV often enough.

"Yes. Who are you?"

"Police, Miss Jannery. Who were you expecting? Dr David Bymeres?"

Chapter 12

THE ROOMS WHICH Ingrid Jannery occupied had been bedrooms in the old days. This was obvious to Masters, who glanced round as he entered her sitting room. The fireplace was hideous—one of the old, box-shaped, bedroom variety, overburdened with cast-iron decorations, but very short on space in which coal might burn. The hearth and surround were in glazed, aspidistra-green tiles: the mantel not wide enough to take a decent clock. But despite this, the room was nicely proportioned and of a fair size, and the occupant had successfully impressed on it something of what Masters supposed must be her own personality.

All the way round the walls was a wooden dado, a yard high, of vertical tongued and grooved planking topped by a cross-plate two inches wide. In the past this would have been stained and grained—the décor so beloved of Victorians because 'it wouldn't show the dirt'. Miss Jannery had it painted basically a dove-grey with a touch of yellow in it, but every seventh strut was in dark wine red relieved with a gold filigree transfer. The idea, Masters supposed, was to give a Regency effect. Whether this had been achieved or not was a matter for doubt, but he didn't find the overall effect unpleasing. He liked another touch she had added. In the middle of each grey area was one of a series of fashion vignettes. A Gainsborough Lady nodded to Brummel, while Prinny eyed the stomacher of the Virgin Queen's best dress with a lack-lustre leer. There were more than a score of these round the room. On the cross-plate were small china dogs of every shape and colour, more numerous than a pack of Exmoor stag hounds. Above the cross-plate, a delicate paper in the same colour as the dado but without the stripes, and here the yellow predominated over the dove-grey. Above this, a gilded picture rail and a cornice that curved into the ceiling. The furniture was modern. Wherever there was wood, it was teak. The seating arrangements were—to Masters—bizarre. He seemed to remember they called the huge cushions, of which there were four on the floor, bean bags. In this room one reclined, and when taking coffee, even from a low table, one had to stretch up to reach it. Fortunately for him and his team there was a convertible divan under the window and a couple of folding garden chairs stacked at the end of what he believed was called a compendium—a long low piece of furniture with numerous holes and gaps to take books, record player, discs and bric-à-brac.

Masters took in the setting before turning to the jewel. Green had been right. She was something! As frail and delicate looking as hand-pinched porcelain was his first impression. She was the text-book goddess of beauty—at first glance. Tall, well-figured, golden-haired and blue-eyed. But the blue eyes were not those of an innocent. There was no reason why they should have been, but even so, Masters felt a stab of dismay, almost of disappointment, when he saw the look in them. He couldn't describe it—it was too complex—wary, calculating, mean, venomous even. He wondered if he wasn't seeing these things there because he expected to do so. Certainly he was aware that had he not been meeting Ingrid Jannery under these circumstances he would have found her physically fascinating.

"Would you like to sit down, Miss Jannery? We may be here for some time."

"Who are you?" she demanded, the colour rising in her cheeks.

"The Scotland Yard team investigating the death of Mrs Bymeres. My name is Masters. I'm a detective superintendent. My colleagues are Inspector Green and Sergeant Hill."

"What has the death of Mrs Bymeres got to do with me?"

"Sit down, please. Hill, bring one of those folding chairs."

She sat as Hill placed the chair for her. She was wearing a skimpy little broderie anglaise blouse that clung to and enhanced her figure. The full denim skirt, though cut to the

179

modern length, did nothing to hide the beauty of her legs as she sat, making no modest attempt to hide her knees.

After a little silence, Masters, who with Green had occupied the divan, said quietly: "For a doctor to divorce a wife who is ill is very difficult."

She didn't reply. She raised her chin as much as to say the matter was of no interest to her.

"For a doctor whose wife is a relative of the senior partner in the practice in which the husband is employed, it is even more difficult."

"I don't know why you are rabbiting on like this. I never asked David Bymeres to divorce his wife."

"I know," murmured Masters quietly.

"What?" asked Green, astounded. "You mean you and he were carrying on here at a merry rate and the question of his divorce never came up? I don't believe it."

"Oh it came up, all right," she replied. "David was always going on about it."

"Getting a divorce so's he could marry you?"

"That's right."

"And you say you didn't encourage him?"

"I did my best to discourage him."

"Why?"

"Because I knew it would never happen. I prefer not to live in a fool's paradise, Mr Green."

Green looked across at Masters who stared back solemnly. "I believe Miss Jannery."

"Oh yeah!"

"Yes." He turned to the girl. "I suppose Dr Bymeres told you that his articles of partnership could be terminated by a majority vote among his colleagues?"

"Yes. He told me that. I suppose he told you that, too."

"No. I haven't questioned the doctor along those lines yet. But it is usual or at any rate not uncommon for such saving clauses in partnerships. It works both ways. Individual doctors are free to leave to take up other appointments should they wish to do so. However, that's beside the point. Dr Bymeres told you that he was certain his colleagues would

180

wish him to go were he to divorce his wife?"

"That's right. He said he wanted a divorce but it was going to create difficulties."

"As you were well aware."

"I told you! I never urged him to get a divorce."

"And I said I knew you hadn't."

"You're a good guesser. Would you mind passing me my handbag from the window sill. I want a cigarette."

Masters realised she had changed the subject to win a break. He was frightening her a little. She was trying to head him off. He waited patiently until the business of passing the bag, lighting the cigarette and handing an ashtray was over. Then—

"A pretty good guesser, Miss Jannery. I guess you are not an unintelligent woman. You were well aware that a doctor who divorces a sick wife and who is then kicked out by his partners might find it difficult to get the sort of practice that would suit you, were you to marry him. Like most of us, doctors need references when applying for jobs. Posts in fashionable areas would not be available to a doctor who had been divorced from a sick wife—after all, doctors are supposed to care for the sick—and whose actions had so upset his colleagues that they had ditched him. Of course he would always be accepted in an under-privileged area where doctors are so hard to get that the Ministry of Health has to offer special inducements to attract medics. But you wouldn't want to live in a slum, even as the wife of a doctor, would you, Miss Jannery?"

"Who would?"

"There's always abroad," suggested Green.

"I'm afraid not," said Masters. "The sort of places which would attract Miss Jannery—the States or Canada for instance —are very particular about whom they accept. They ask for references, too. Good ones. Not ones which say that the writer has found the person referred to as being so short on human kindness that his erstwhile colleagues ended the partnership because of it. Am I right, Miss Jannery?"

"Perfectly. As I said, I never encouraged David to divorce his wife."

"I see that," murmured Green. "How did you get to know him?"

"I got flu last January. I'd been on their list for a couple of years—ever since I moved here—but I'd never had to use them. But when I got flu, I croaked a message into the phone and about an hour later David arrived. He called again the next day."

"As soon as that?"

"To bring me my medicine. I couldn't go to the chemist myself and there was nobody. . . ."

"I get it," said Green. "The doc played errand boy even in the busy season, just to see you again."

"You can put what interpretation you like on his actions."

"I will. So you became mates. Bed-mates!"

"If you want to be that crude, yes."

"Don't try to make me blush," replied Green. "I'm uninsultable."

"I'm sure."

"So, Miss Jannery, you never urged Dr Bymeres to divorce his wife," said Masters, pacifically.

"I've said so."

"And I believe you. But Dr Bymeres was in love with you and wanted to marry you."

"Yes. He was always going on about it."

"Tell me, did you actively discourage him from divorce?"

"Of course I did. I pointed out much the same things as you have. He thought life in a slum would be all right as long as I was there with him. I knew it wouldn't be."

"Because, I suggest, you didn't love him, did you, Miss Jannery?"

"Oh, hell! Love! Of course I didn't love him. Not all that hearts and flowers stuff. He was okay. But I didn't want a husband who'd be called out of bed every night and who'd come home half dead and smelling of vomit. David was all right as a man, but not as a husband."

"That's what I thought."

"Thought what?"

"That you never told David Bymeres you didn't love him."

182

He could tell he'd made his point. She paused momentarily before replying.

"Why should I? I've said I liked him. What would you expect me to do?"

"Exactly what you appeared to have done. You never told him you didn't love him. Did you, in fact, suggest that you *did* love him, safe in the knowledge that you would never have to marry him because divorce, for him, was unthinkable?"

"Well...."

"When you were in bed together, Miss Jannery? Making love and murmuring endearments? Motivated by the pleasure he gave you and leaning heavily on the knowledge that you would never have to redeem any pledge of love you might make?"

"I suppose so."

"You know so. Didn't you realise what a dangerous game you were playing?"

"Dangerous? We went to bed together, that's all."

"It isn't all, Miss Jannery. David Bymeres was besotted with you. You are a beautiful woman. A perfect woman in his eyes. Everything his wife was not. And you told him you returned his love. He wanted to marry you. He was entitled to suppose *you* wanted to marry him. But there was one barrier. His wife. He couldn't divorce her. He knew that such a step would have its disadvantages even if you would agree to marry him after that, but you urged him not to sue for divorce. You left him in no doubt you loved him but would not marry to live in a slum or an African jungle. So the way of divorce was closed to him. What other way was there to get rid of the barrier that stood between him and his heart's desire? The barrier of a sick wife who couldn't be divorced? There could only be one way. She must die. Apparently by accident or by her own hand or from natural causes—any way, in fact, that would not overtly involve Bymeres himself, and so would not affect his career. He had to make that happen because it was his only way of getting you, Miss Jannery. So far, because you were his patient, he had to visit you

183

clandestinely. Nobody had been allowed to know of your relationship. But once his wife was dead....

"He planned to do it, Miss Jannery, because you allowed him to believe you loved him. Had you not done so, had he been made aware of the fact that your relationship was just a transient affair, he would never have gone to those lengths. But he thought *he* had everything to win as long as *his wife* lost her life."

"You're blaming me. I didn't know he would...."

"Would what?"

"You've almost been saying he killed her."

"Almost? What did he tell you this last weekend when he came to see you?"

"That she died in her sleep."

"That would be a shock to you."

"It was. A double one. The shock of her death, and...."

"And the shock of realising that Bymeres would now be claiming his pound of flesh: that he'd expect you to marry him after a decent interval?"

"Yes. I stopped him from ... well, with his wife just dead ... it didn't seem right."

"I know. But you do see, Miss Jannery, don't you, that though you were in no way to blame for Mrs Bymeres' death, a word from you could have saved her? Because he did kill her, you know, in order to be free to marry you."

"I couldn't have known he would do it."

"Perhaps not."

"What do you mean, perhaps?"

Masters stood up. "I would have thought that a woman so schooled in the ways of men, as you with your great beauty must be, would have realised that a passion such as Bymeres must have held for you might be dangerous."

He was looking straight at her. As he watched he saw her eyes brim with tears. He was pleased. A sign of remorse at last. But he was not prepared for her next few words.

"It was," she said, trying to keep the tears from coming. "I knew it was. But I thought it would be dangerous to me, not to her."

"He threatened you?"

"No, no. Never. But I sometimes got the feeling that if ever I ... told him I didn't love him ... oh, hell, it was part of what made it for me."

"The danger?"

"Not exactly."

"The feeling that he would go to any lengths—even to harming you—in order not to lose your love?"

"Yes. It was ... exciting, I suppose."

Green grunted. "You misread it lady. It was his wife who got the chop."

"Only because ... well, what would have happened to me if I'd said I didn't love him?"

Masters signalled to Hill. "Try and find a drink for Miss Jannery." Then he turned again to her. "Don't blame yourself, Miss Jannery. I'm willing to believe that you were in as much danger as Mrs Bymeres."

Chapter 13

"So that's that," said Green, as they left the house. "Nothing to take her in for."

"Nothing. No incitement to murder. And even if we suspected it, we'd never get it to stick. Nobody would believe that a comparatively empty-headed girl could persuade a doctor—a much more mature and intelligent person—to commit murder against his will."

"Not in so many words perhaps," said Hill, "but that figure of hers could incite any man to anything."

"Rubbish."

"Any man who was gone on her."

"I felt her power," admitted Masters. "Just for a moment when we first met her. And at the time I was regarding her as murderess, more or less."

"You knew," accused Green. "You knew all along what the score was."

"I swear I didn't. Only after I saw her. I just knew that a girl like that would never contemplate being a general practitioner's wife. And I reckoned she'd never say she would. But it was obvious she hadn't rebuffed Bymeres, or he wouldn't have still thought he had a chance. It was only then that I saw the score. She didn't have to rebuff him. She knew she was safe because of his wife."

"And the bit about the danger to herself?"

"I must say that came as a complete surprise. But why shouldn't it be true? He was prepared to take life to get her, why shouldn't he be prepared to do something to stop somebody else getting her—if he couldn't have her himself?"

Green scratched his head. "I can imagine him not liking to be thwarted."

"Where to, chief?" asked Hill as they got into the car.

Masters turned to Green. "I've got a supper appointment. That's why I told Wrotham I'd wrap it up tomorrow morning. But if you and Hill would rather go ahead tonight...."

"With or without you?"

"I'd rather not miss my supper."

"Look, chief," said Hill. "I appreciate what you're suggesting. You want me to do it on my own—for experience before I go. Oh, I know the DI would be there to hold my hand, but quite honestly, I'd rather you did it yourself tomorrow."

"Me, too," said Green. "Besides, why should I miss my dinner on Bymeres' account?"

"Suit yourselves," said Masters. "Make as good time as you can, Sergeant. I'm running a bit late."

"One point we haven't mentioned," said Green.

"I know," replied Masters. "Why did Bymeres tell us about that leaflet?"

Hill grunted. "That's it. It seemed a daft thing to do. So why do it?"

"Because he knew we would discover it sooner or later, and he wanted to score a point with us for his own candour and magnanimity towards Spiller."

"Right. Then why didn't Spiller mention it instead of crucifying himself for not having spelled it out to Mrs Bymeres?"

"I can only guess the answer to that. It's this. Mrs Bymeres' death was an avoidable tragedy. Avoidable if she had been adequately informed about the prohibited foods. It was her doctor's job to inform her. Spiller didn't do so. So he lost a patient. Oh, yes, the pharmacist usually puts a leaflet in the prescription. But forget that. It is not the pharmacist's legal job to caution patients. His job is to provide what the doctor orders—even to query the prescription if the doctor makes a mistake in strengths or amounts of drugs. But there the responsibility ends, except perhaps for writing how much and how many times a day the patient should take the drug. So Spiller—whose responsibility it was—relied on a man whose responsibility it was not, to inform the patient. The odds against tragedy occurring because of this mistake on Spiller's part are immense. But the tragedy did happen.

187

Spiller is the type of man to accept the responsibility for it to the point where he will come to us and admit it. But he would never allow it to be thought that he would implicate the pharmacist in any way. And the surest way of not implicating Blundell was to avoid mentioning him or the leaflet.

"Naturally, Spiller would wonder about the leaflet, but who could he ask to tell him if she had received it? The best person—Mrs Bymeres—was dead. Could he ask Blundell? Always assuming that he knew Mrs Bymeres patronised Blundell, could he honestly ring up a professional man and ask him if he had supplied the dead woman with the usual leaflet which, if handed to her, would have saved her life? What would Blundell's reply be?"

"Knowing the woman to be dead, he would say yes," argued Hill. "She wasn't about any longer to deny it, so whether he had or not, he would say he had."

"Either that or he could plead, at worst, that he was sure he did, but he couldn't be expected to remember a small transaction which took place at a busy time over a week earlier. So Spiller guessed he would get no real joy there. The only other person who might know would be Bymeres, the dead woman's husband. In view of the fact that the tragedy must have shrieked of a medical killing, the last person Spiller could have approached would be Bymeres, the likeliest medical man to be implicated."

"So Spiller's best line was to come to us, admit his responsibility and say nothing of the leaflet?"

"I believe so. At any rate, that's what I would have done, knowing that the police would eventually get round to hearing of the leaflet and subsequently tracing it."

"We'll check on it," yawned Green. "Spiller will give us a lecture on it."

The car sped on through more open country. Even so it was almost nine before it set Masters down at the gate of Pilgrim's Cottage.

The front door was open. He walked straight in to the unlit sitting room.

"Did you think I wasn't coming?"

She was seated in a chair with her back to him. Without looking round, she said. "I knew you would come. You promised."

He rounded the chair. She was dressed in a faded-blue denim trouser suit. She took his hands and he lifted her to her feet.

"All over?" she asked.

"No," he said, as he took her in his arms. "It's just beginning."

"Don't let's play misunderstandings."

"As you wish. Do you understand this?"

She understood well enough judging by the way she responded to the kiss.

A little later—

"Still no misunderstandings? Right. How soon will you marry me, Wanda?"

She looked up at him.

"Change the name and not the letter, change for worse and not for better," she quoted.

"You mean change Mace to Masters? Rubbish. You were not born Mace."

"Née Goodyear, actually."

"There you are then. G to M."

She shook her head. "I took that exact step once before. I try not to repeat my mistakes."

"So do I. This—exactly this—has happened to me before. Last time I couldn't change her mind. This time I intend to succeed."

She looked up at him.

"Supper's ready."

THE PERENNIAL LIBRARY MYSTERY SERIES

Ted Allbeury

THE OTHER SIDE OF SILENCE   P 669, $2.84
"In the best le Carré tradition . . . an ingenious and readable book."
—New York Times Book Review

PALOMINO BLONDE   P 670, $2.84
"Fast-moving, splendidly technocratic intercontinental espionage tale
. . . you'll love it."   *—The Times* (London)

SNOWBALL   P 671, $2.84
"A novel of byzantine intrigue. . . ."*—New York Times Book Review*

Delano Ames

CORPSE DIPLOMATIQUE   P 637, $2.84
"Sprightly and intelligent."
—New York Herald Tribune Book Review

FOR OLD CRIME'S SAKE   P 629, $2.84

MURDER, MAESTRO, PLEASE   P 630, $2.84
"If there is a more engaging couple in modern fiction than Jane and
Dagobert Brown, we have not met them."   *—Scotsman*

SHE SHALL HAVE MURDER   P 638, $2.84
"Combines the merit of both the English and American schools in the
new mystery. It's as breezy as the best of the American ones, and has
the sophistication and wit of any top-notch Britisher."
—New York Herald Tribune Book Review

E. C. Bentley

TRENT'S LAST CASE   P 440, $2.50
"One of the three best detective stories ever written."
—Agatha Christie

TRENT'S OWN CASE   P 516, $2.25
"I won't waste time saying that the plot is sound and the detection
satisfying. Trent has not altered a scrap and reappears with all his old
humor and charm."   *—Dorothy L. Sayers*

Andrew Bergman

THE BIG KISS-OFF OF 1944 P 673, $2.84

"It is without doubt the nearest thing to genuine Chandler I've ever come across. . . . Tough, witty—very witty—and a beautiful eye for period detail. . . ."
—Jack Higgins

HOLLYWOOD AND LEVINE P 674, $2.84

"Fast-paced private-eye fiction." —*San Francisco Chronicle*

Gavin Black

A DRAGON FOR CHRISTMAS P 473, $1.95

"Potent excitement!" —*New York Herald Tribune*

THE EYES AROUND ME P 485, $1.95

"I stayed up until all hours last night reading *The Eyes Around Me*, which is something I do not do very often, but I was so intrigued by the ingeniousness of Mr. Black's plotting and the witty way in which he spins his mystery. I can only say that I enjoyed the book enormously."
—F. van Wyck Mason

YOU WANT TO DIE, JOHNNY? P 472, $1.95

"Gavin Black doesn't just develop a pressure plot in suspense, he adds uninfected wit, character, charm, and sharp knowledge of the Far East to make rereading as keen as the first race-through." —*Book Week*

Nicholas Blake

THE CORPSE IN THE SNOWMAN P 427, $1.95

"If there is a distinction between the novel and the detective story (which we do not admit), then this book deserves a high place in both categories." —*New York Times*

END OF CHAPTER P 397, $1.95

". . . admirably solid . . . an adroit formal detective puzzle backed up by firm characterization and a knowing picture of London publishing."
—*New York Times*

HEAD OF A TRAVELER P 398, $2.25

"Another grade A detective story of the right old jigsaw persuasion."
—*New York Herald Tribune Book Review*

MINUTE FOR MURDER P 419, $1.95

"An outstanding mystery novel. Mr. Blake's writing is a delight in itself." —*New York Times*

THE MORNING AFTER DEATH P 520, $1.95

"One of Blake's best." —Rex Warner

A PENKNIFE IN MY HEART   P 521, $2.25
"Style brilliant . . . and suspenseful."   —*San Francisco Chronicle*

THE PRIVATE WOUND   P 531, $2.25
"[Blake's] best novel in a dozen years . . . . An intensely penetrating study
of sexual passion. . . . A powerful story of murder and its aftermath."
                                    —Anthony Boucher, *New York Times*

A QUESTION OF PROOF   P 494, $1.95
"The characters in this story are unusually well drawn, and the suspense
is well sustained."   —*New York Times*

THE SAD VARIETY   P 495, $2.25
"It is a stunner. I read it instead of eating, instead of sleeping."
                                    —Dorothy Salisbury Davis

THERE'S TROUBLE BREWING   P 569, $3.37
"Nigel Strangeways is a puzzling mixture of simplicity and penetration,
but all the more real for that."
                                    —*The Times* (London) *Literary Supplement*

THOU SHELL OF DEATH   P 428, $1.95
"It has all the virtues of culture, intelligence and sensibility that the most
exacting connoisseur could ask of detective fiction."
                                    —*The Times* (London) *Literary Supplement*

THE WIDOW'S CRUISE   P 399, $2.25
"A stirring suspense. . . . The thrilling tale leaves nothing to be desired."
                                    —*Springfield Republican*

Oliver Bleeck

THE BRASS GO-BETWEEN   P 645, $2.84
"Fiction with a flair, well above the norm for thrillers."
                                    —*Associated Press*

THE PROCANE CHRONICLE   P 647, $2.84
"Without peer in American suspense."   —*Los Angeles Times*

PROTOCOL FOR A KIDNAPPING   P 646, $2.84
"The zigzags of plot are electric; the characters sharp; but it is the wit
and irony and touches of plain fun which make the whole a standout."
                                    —*Los Angeles Times*

John & Emery Bonett

A BANNER FOR PEGASUS   P 554, $2.40

"A gem! Beautifully plotted and set. . . . Not only is the murder adroit and deserved, and the detection competent, but the love story is charming."   —Jacques Barzun and Wendell Hertig Taylor

DEAD LION   P 563, $2.40

"A clever plot, authentic background and interesting characters highly recommended this one."   —*New Republic*

THE SOUND OF MURDER   P 642, $2.84

The suspects are many, the clues few, but the gentle Inspector ferrets out the truth and pursues the case to its bitter and shocking end.

Christianna Brand

GREEN FOR DANGER   P 551, $2.50

"You have to reach for the greatest of Great Names (Christie, Carr, Queen . . .) to find Brand's rivals in the devious subtleties of the trade."
                          —Anthony Boucher

TOUR DE FORCE   P 572, $2.40

"Complete with traps for the over-ingenious, a double-reverse surprise ending and a key clue planted so fairly and obviously that you completely overlook it. If that's your idea of perfect entertainment, then seize at once upon *Tour de Force.*"   —Anthony Boucher, *New York Times*

James Byrom

OR BE HE DEAD   P 585, $2.84

"A very original tale . . . Well written and steadily entertaining."
—Jacques Barzun and Wendell Hertig Taylor, *A Catalogue of Crime*

Henry Calvin

IT'S DIFFERENT ABROAD   P 640, $2.84

"What is remarkable and delightful, Mr. Calvin imparts a flavor of satire to what he renovates and compels us to take straight."

                          —Jacques Barzun

Marjorie Carleton

VANISHED   P 559, $2.40

"Exceptional . . . a minor triumph."
—Jacques Barzun and Wendell Hertig Taylor, *A Catalogue of Crime*

George Harmon Coxe

MURDER WITH PICTURES   P 527, $2.25

"[Coxe] has hit the bull's-eye with his first shot."

        —*New York Times*

Edmund Crispin

BURIED FOR PLEASURE   P 506, $2.50

"Absolute and unalloyed delight."

        —Anthony Boucher, *New York Times*

Lionel Davidson

THE MENORAH MEN   P 592, $2.84

"Of his fellow thriller writers, only John Le Carré shows the same instinct for the viscera."   —*Chicago Tribune*

NIGHT OF WENCESLAS   P 595, $2.84

"A most ingenious thriller, so enriched with style, wit, and a sense of serious comedy that it all but transcends its kind."

        —*The New Yorker*

THE ROSE OF TIBET   P 593, $2.84

"I hadn't realized how much I missed the genuine Adventure story . . . until I read *The Rose of Tibet*."   —Graham Greene

D. M. Devine

MY BROTHER'S KILLER   P 558, $2.40

"A most enjoyable crime story which I enjoyed reading down to the last moment."   —Agatha Christie

Kenneth Fearing

THE BIG CLOCK   P 500, $1.95

"It will be some time before chill-hungry clients meet again so rare a compound of irony, satire, and icy-fingered narrative. *The Big Clock* is . . . a psychothriller you won't put down."   —*Weekly Book Review*

Andrew Garve

THE ASHES OF LODA   P 430, $1.50

"Garve . . . embellishes a fine fast adventure story with a more credible picture of the U.S.S.R. than is offered in most thrillers."

        —*New York Times Book Review*

THE CUCKOO LINE AFFAIR   P 451, $1.95

". . . an agreeable and ingenious piece of work."   —*The New Yorker*

C. W. Grafton (cont'd)

THE RAT BEGAN TO GNAW THE ROPE   P 639, $2.84
"Fast, humorous story with flashes of brilliance."

—The New Yorker

Edward Grierson

THE SECOND MAN   P 528, $2.25
"One of the best trial-testimony books to have come along in quite a
while."   *—The New Yorker*

Bruce Hamilton

TOO MUCH OF WATER   P 635, $2.84
"A superb sea mystery. . . . The prose is excellent."
—Jacques Barzun and Wendell Hertig Taylor, *A Catalogue of Crime*

Cyril Hare

DEATH IS NO SPORTSMAN   P 555, $2.40
"You will be thrilled because it succeeds in placing an ingenious story
in a new and refreshing setting. . . . The identity of the murderer is really
a surprise."   *—Daily Mirror*

DEATH WALKS THE WOODS   P 556, $2.40
"Here is a fine formal detective story, with a technically brilliant solution
demanding the attention of all connoisseurs of construction."
                    —Anthony Boucher, *New York Times Book Review*

AN ENGLISH MURDER   P 455, $2.50
"By a long shot, the best crime story I have read for a long time.
Everything is traditional, but originality does not suffer. The setting is
perfect. Full marks to Mr. Hare."   *—Irish Press*

SUICIDE EXCEPTED   P 636, $2.84
"Adroit in its manipulation . . . and distinguished by a plot-twister which
I'll wager Christie wishes she'd thought of."   *—New York Times*

TENANT FOR DEATH   P 570, $2.84
"The way in which an air of probability is combined both with clear,
terse narrative and with a good deal of subtle suburban atmosphere,
proves the extreme skill of the writer."   *—The Spectator*

TRAGEDY AT LAW   P 522, $2.25
"An extremely urbane and well-written detective story."

—New York Times

UNTIMELY DEATH P 514, $2.25

"The English detective story at its quiet best, meticulously underplayed, rich in perceivings of the droll human animal and ready at the last with a neat surprise which has been there all the while had we but wits to see it." —*New York Herald Tribune Book Review*

THE WIND BLOWS DEATH P 589, $2.84

"A plot compounded of musical knowledge, a Dickens allusion, and a subtle point in law is related with delightfully unobtrusive wit, warmth, and style." —*New York Times*

WITH A BARE BODKIN P 523, $2.25

"One of the best detective stories published for a long time."

—*The Spectator*

Robert Harling

THE ENORMOUS SHADOW P 545, $2.50

"In some ways the best spy story of the modern period. . . . The writing is terse and vivid . . . the ending full of action . . . altogether first-rate."
—Jacques Barzun and Wendell Hertig Taylor, *A Catalogue of Crime*

Matthew Head

THE CABINDA AFFAIR P 541, $2.25

"An absorbing whodunit and a distinguished novel of atmosphere."
—Anthony Boucher, *New York Times*

THE CONGO VENUS P 597, $2.84

"Terrific. The dialogue is just plain wonderful." —*Boston Globe*

MURDER AT THE FLEA CLUB P 542, $2.50

"The true delight is in Head's style, its limpid ease combined with humor and an awesome precision of phrase." —*San Francisco Chronicle*

M. V. Heberden

ENGAGED TO MURDER P 533, $2.25

"Smooth plotting." —*New York Times*

James Hilton

WAS IT MURDER? P 501, $1.95

"The story is well planned and well written." —*New York Times*

S. B. Hough

DEAR DAUGHTER DEAD   P 661, $2.84
"A highly intelligent and sophisticated story of police detection . . . not
to be missed on any account."   —Francis Iles, *The Guardian*

SWEET SISTER SEDUCED   P 662, $2.84
In the course of a nightlong conversation between the Inspector and the
suspect, the complex emotions of a very strange marriage are revealed.

P. M. Hubbard

HIGH TIDE   P 571, $2.40
"A smooth elaboration of mounting horror and danger."

—*Library Journal*

Elspeth Huxley

THE AFRICAN POISON MURDERS   P 540, $2.25
"Obscure venom, manical mutilations, deadly bush fire, thrilling climax
compose major opus.... Top-flight."

—*Saturday Review of Literature*

MURDER ON SAFARI   P 587, $2.84
"Right now we'd call Mrs. Huxley a dangerous rival to Agatha Christie."   —*Books*

Francis Iles

BEFORE THE FACT   P 517, $2.50
"Not many 'serious' novelists have produced character studies to compare with Iles's internally terrifying portrait of the murderer in *Before
the Fact,* his masterpiece and a work truly deserving the appellation of
unique and beyond price."   —Howard Haycraft

MALICE AFORETHOUGHT   P 532, $1.95
"It is a long time since I have read anything so good as *Malice Aforethought,* with its cynical humour, acute criminology, plausible detail and
rapid movement. It makes you hug yourself with pleasure."
—H. C. Harwood, *Saturday Review*

Michael Innes

APPLEBY ON ARARAT   P 648, $2.84
"Superbly plotted and humorously written."   —*The New Yorker*

APPLEBY'S END   P 649, $2.84
"Most amusing."   —*Boston Globe*

THE CASE OF THE JOURNEYING BOY P 632, $3.12
"I could see no faults in it. There is no one to compare with him."
—*Illustrated London News*

DEATH ON A QUIET DAY P 677, $2.84
"Delightfully witty." —*Chicago Sunday Tribune*

DEATH BY WATER P 574, $2.40
"The amount of ironic social criticism and deft characterization of scenes and people would serve another author for six books."
—Jacques Barzun and Wendell Hertig Taylor

HARE SITTING UP P 590, $2.84
"There is hardly anyone (in mysteries or mainstream) more exquisitely literate, allusive and Jamesian—and hardly anyone with a firmer sense of melodramatic plot or a more vigorous gift of storytelling."
—Anthony Boucher, *New York Times*

THE LONG FAREWELL P 575, $2.40
"A model of the deft, classic detective story, told in the most wittily diverting prose." —*New York Times*

THE MAN FROM THE SEA P 591, $2.84
"The pace is brisk, the adventures exciting and excitingly told, and above all he keeps to the very end the interesting ambiguity of the man from the sea." —*New Statesman*

ONE MAN SHOW P 672, $2.84
"Exciting, amusingly written . . . very good enjoyment it is."
—*The Spectator*

THE SECRET VANGUARD P 584, $2.84
"Innes . . . has mastered the art of swift, exciting and well-organized narrative." —*New York Times*

THE WEIGHT OF THE EVIDENCE P 633, $2.84
"First-class puzzle, deftly solved. University background interesting and amusing." —*Saturday Review of Literature*

Mary Kelly

THE SPOILT KILL P 565, $2.40
"Mary Kelly is a new Dorothy Sayers. . . . [An] exciting new novel."
—*Evening News*

Lange Lewis

THE BIRTHDAY MURDER   P 518, $1.95

"Almost perfect in its playlike purity and delightful prose."
— Jacques Barzun and Wendell Hertig Taylor

Allan MacKinnon

HOUSE OF DARKNESS   P 582, $2.84

"His best . . . a perfect compendium."
— Jacques Barzun and Wendell Hertig Taylor, *A Catalogue of Crime*

Frank Parrish

FIRE IN THE BARLEY   P 651, $2.84

"A remarkable and brilliant first novel. . . . entrancing."
— *The Spectator*

SNARE IN THE DARK   P 650, $2.84

The wily English poacher Dan Mallett is framed for murder and has to confront unknown enemies to clear himself.

STING OF THE HONEYBEE   P 652, $2.84

"Terrorism and murder visit a sleepy English village in this witty, offbeat thriller."
— *Chicago Sun-Times*

Austin Ripley

MINUTE MYSTERIES   P 387, $2.50

More than one hundred of the world's shortest detective stories. Only one possible solution to each case!

Thomas Sterling

THE EVIL OF THE DAY   P 529, $2.50

"Prose as witty and subtle as it is sharp and clear. . .characters unconventionally conceived and richly bodied forth . . . . In short, a novel to be treasured."
— Anthony Boucher, *New York Times*

Julian Symons

THE BELTING INHERITANCE   P 468, $1.95

"A superb whodunit in the best tradition of the detective story."
— August Derleth, *Madison Capital Times*

BOGUE'S FORTUNE   P 481, $1.95

"There's a touch of the old sardonic humour, and more than a touch of style."
— *The Spectator*

THE COLOR OF MURDER
P 461, $1.95

"A singularly unostentatious and memorably brilliant detective story."
—*New York Herald Tribune Book Review*

Dorothy Stockbridge Tillet
(John Stephen Strange)

THE MAN WHO KILLED FORTESCUE
P 536, $2.25

"Better than average."
—*Saturday Review of Literature*

Simon Troy

THE ROAD TO RHUINE
P 583, $2.84

"Unusual and agreeably told."
—*San Francisco Chronicle*

SWIFT TO ITS CLOSE
P 546, $2.40

"A nicely literate British mystery . . . the atmosphere and the plot are exceptionally well wrought, the dialogue excellent."
—*Best Sellers*

Henry Wade

THE DUKE OF YORK'S STEPS
P 588, $2.84

"A classic of the golden age."
—Jacques Barzun and Wendell Hertig Taylor, *A Catalogue of Crime*

A DYING FALL
P 543, $2.50

"One of those expert British suspense jobs . . . it crackles with undercurrents of blackmail, violent passion and murder. Topnotch in its class."
—*Time*

THE HANGING CAPTAIN
P 548, $2.50

"This is a detective story for connoisseurs, for those who value clear thinking and good writing above mere ingenuity and easy thrills."
—*The Times* (London) *Literary Supplement*

Hillary Waugh

LAST SEEN WEARING . . .
P 552, $2.40

"A brilliant tour de force."
—Julian Symons

THE MISSING MAN
P 553, $2.40

"The quiet detailed police work of Chief Fred C. Fellows, Stockford, Conn., is at its best in *The Missing Man* . . . one of the Chief's toughest cases and one of the best handled."
—Anthony Boucher, *New York Times Book Review*

Henry Kitchell Webster

WHO IS THE NEXT?   P 539, $2.25
"A double murder, private-plane piloting, a neat impersonation, and a delicate courtship are adroitly combined by a writer who knows how to use the language."   —Jacques Barzun and Wendell Hertig Taylor

John Welcome

GO FOR BROKE   P 663, $2.84
A rich financier chases Richard Graham half 'round Europe in a desperate attempt to prevent the truth getting out.

RUN FOR COVER   P 664, $2.84
"I can think of few writers in the international intrigue game with such a gift for fast and vivid storytelling."
                                        —New York Times Book Review

STOP AT NOTHING   P 665, $2.84
"Mr. Welcome is lively, vivid and highly readable."
                                        —New York Times Book Review

Anna Mary Wells

MURDERER'S CHOICE   P 534, $2.50
"Good writing, ample action, and excellent character work."
                                        —Saturday Review of Literature

A TALENT FOR MURDER   P 535, $2.25
"The discovery of the villain is a decided shock."   —Books

Charles Williams

DEAD CALM   P 655, $2.84
"A brilliant tour de force of inventive plotting, fine manipulation of a small cast and breathtaking sequences of spectacular navigation."
                                        —New York Times Book Review

THE SAILCLOTH SHROUD   P 654, $2.84
"A fine novel of excitement, spirited, fresh and satisfying."
                                        —New York Times

THE WRONG VENUS   P 656, $2.84
Swindler Lawrence Colby and the lovely Martine create a story of romance, larceny, and very blunt homicide.

**If you enjoyed this book you'll want to know about
THE PERENNIAL LIBRARY MYSTERY SERIES**
Buy them at your local bookstore or use this coupon for ordering:

Qty	P number	Price

postage and handling charge $1.00
_____ book(s) @ $0.25 _____

TOTAL [   ]

**Prices contained in this coupon are Harper & Row invoice prices only.
They are subject to change without notice, and in no way reflect the prices at
which these books may be sold by other suppliers.**

**HARPER & ROW, Mail Order Dept. #PMS, 10 East 53rd St., New
York, N.Y. 10022.**
Please send me the books I have checked above. I am enclosing $_____
which includes a postage and handling charge of $1.00 for the first book and
25¢ for each additional book. Send check or money order. No cash or
C.O.D.s please

Name_____

Address_____

City_____State_____Zip_____
Please allow 4 weeks for delivery. USA only. This offer expires 12/31/85
Please add applicable sales tax.